ESCAPE THE WAR

PRIYANKA NAMBIAR

ESCAPE THE WAR

MACKENZIE PRESS

www.mackenzie-press.com

ISBN 978-1-7334619-3-1

PROLOGUE

"Five hundred and forty-four, five hundred and forty-five…" Our voices blend together, excitement breaking through our calm appearances. It is late August, and my best friend and I are on a mission: a mission to beat the world record for longest ping-pong rally. The record is one thousand, six hundred, and eighty-seven hits. We have done four hundred. In other words, we have a long way to go.

"*Ugh*. This is taking forever! Can I go? The camera is still running," my younger brother, Chad, whines. I roll my eyes and spit out a quick yes, being careful to keep my eyes focused on the ball. He sprints up the basement stairs, his feet slamming down loudly. I can hear my mom's chastisement from all the way upstairs. I catch Jane's eye, and we both grin. I would be happy watching paint dry with Jane. She is my other half; we do everything together. Jane is like the sister I never had.

I have known Jane my entire life. Ever since we were itty-bitty toddlers, we knew that our friendship was something special. She just… *knows*. Whenever I am feeling sad, Jane is the one who makes me smile. Whenever I am stressed, Jane is the one who makes me laugh. Jane is one of the kindest people I have ever known, and I am forever grateful that she has found her way into my life. Without Jane, where would I be in my life now? That's a question I don't really want to answer.

"Careful!" Jane says, raising her voice nervously. I roll my eyes with a hint of playfulness.

"PLEASE. YOU'RE THE ONE WHO'S going to miss it!" I challenge, causing both of us to giggle. A few hours of teasing, laughing, and close calls later, we are almost to the record number of hits. I focus all my attention on hitting the ball. There is no way we're going to screw this up now.

"Three more! Two more!" I count down enthusiastically. I didn't think we actually were going to do it! Jane is nearly jumping out of happiness. But it isn't over yet.

"One—" I pause as Jane flails her arms, stretching for the ball. She almost smashes into the wall and somehow ends up on the floor. The ball lands right beside her and bounces up and down. We both look down at the ball before meeting each other's eyes. I shrug my shoulders and smile. Jane mouths the words "oh well," then bursts out laughing. There goes three hours of ping-pong playing.

She glances at me with a mischievous glimmer in her eyes.

"Okay, so I may have missed the ball, but at least I didn't follow you around in preschool like a *stalker!* I mean, I guess I can finally forgive you for that now that I screwed up." Jane smirks, a mischievous fire glittering in her eyes. I gasp, pretending to look offended.

"What does that have to do with anything? I should be the one forgiving *you*, little miss know-it-all! And come on, you wanted to be my friend anyway. I mean, who could resist this face?" I strike a dramatic pose while fighting my urge to laugh. Jane rolls her eyes and playfully shoves me out of my stance.

"Hey! I thought third-grade Jane 'didn't believe in pushing,' huh?" I mock as memories of a tiny little Jane preaching about the importance of not pushing resurface. Jane blushes.

"That was a phase!" she cries. I burst into a fit of giggles, and Jane joins me. We spend the next hour making fun of each other using our childhood memories. Let's just say that Jane and I together were a *big* handful. I guess nothing has changed.

"C'mon! My mom has popsicles upstairs!" I exclaim after our memories finally run dry. Jane perks up, and we grin. Still giggling, we race each other upstairs and burst through the door. "Hi mom!" I chirp. Jane smiles widely and waves. My mom tucks a piece of her hair behind her ear and looks up skeptically. She is met with our pleading stares.

"They're in the bottom left of the freezer," she says, smiling. Jane and I share a grin.

"Thanks, mom!" I say sweetly. Jane and I run towards the freezer and throw it open, grabbing our favorite flavors. Jane shields her popsicle with her hand and I give her a questioning look.

"Well? What's my favorite flavor?" Jane asks expectantly. I roll my eyes.

"Is that even a question? Only *you* like grape-flavored popsicles!" Jane removes the hand that obstructed my view to reveal the deep purple color.

"Not bad." I stick my tongue out at her and she laughs. We grab our popsicles and head out the front door to make it in time for sunset. Our chaotic energy has started to die down, leaving us in a more contemplative mood.

"I can't believe summer is over," Jane says sadly. I nod. It feels like school just ended yesterday.

"But it's okay! We can still hang out during the school year. Remember our school-night sleepover?" I add, with a fake grimace. Jane seems to brighten a little, and she lets out a laugh.

"'Staying up all night was very immature of you, young lady! You are grounded!'" I say, mocking our mothers' stern reactions from last year.

"We *totally* did not fall asleep at all during the day," Jane responds. I smile.

We sure do have a lot of memories together. I'm sure this year is going to bring many more. The door creaks open behind us, and we turn in surprise.

"Dad!" I envelop him in a hug and he plants a kiss on my forehead.

"Hey sweetie! Hi Jane!" he responds, giving Jane a smile. At this point, my parents think of Jane as a second daughter. "I was just going to tell you two that dinner is ready. Jane, you're welcome to stay if you'd like!" I glance at Jane and give her an encouraging nod.

Before Jane can reply, her phone beeps loudly. She picks it up, listens for a few seconds, and hangs up.

"Mom says I've got to come home and get ready for school tomorrow. Thank you for the offer, though." My dad nods understandingly and says goodbye before going back inside.

"See you tomorrow!" Jane says with reluctance. I frown and squeeze her tightly, then stick out my left hand expectantly.

"Ahem!" I cough. Jane turns around, apologizes for forgetting, and extends her left hand into mine.

"Up! Down! Left and right! Together we will be all right!" Our hands intertwine in a complex set of gestures choreographed by our younger selves. Jane chuckles quietly.

"We were so dumb back then! '*All right* totally rhymes with *right*, Ivy!'" she says, mimicking herself as a child. I laugh.

We promise to meet each other tomorrow at the flagpole by the entrance of the school. I close the door behind me as she leaves, still waving goodbye. Once the door shuts, I let out a sad sigh.

These past few months have been so much fun! I'm not quite ready to say goodbye to summer yet.

I wake up the next morning excited for a fresh start. Even though I'm disappointed that summer is over, I can't wait to start the day. I'm a high-schooler now! This is it—the start of a new chapter of my life.

I put on my pre-picked outfit while calmly reciting my schedule in my head. English first period, geography second period, art next. I continue to practice the order of my classes in my thoughts as I smooth out my new dress. I glance at myself in the mirror and nod approvingly at my tidy appearance. I have a feeling this year is going to be really special.

My mom yells for me from downstairs, and I quickly throw my hair into a slick high ponytail. I fly down the stairs and grab a granola bar. My mom hastily kisses me goodbye and I start my walk to school. I text Jane to say that I'm on my way, as usual, but oddly, there is no reply. I think nothing of it and continue walking. Wow— first day of freshman year. I know high school is supposed to be awesome, but I'm also kind of terrified. All of the homework, upperclassmen, and endless hallways; something is bound to go wrong! At least Jane and I have each other, because this year is going to be rough.

I reach our meeting spot not much later and scroll through Instagram for the next few minutes while I munch on my granola bar. I'm doing everything in my power to distract myself from my growing nerves. My excitement is turning to worry with every second that passes.

What if I get lost? Or I can't open my locker? What happens if I can't find Jane at lunch? I shake my head to clear my worrisome thoughts and resume my mindless scrolling.

Jane should be here soon. The area around me is becoming more crowded as preppy freshmen begin arriving. Everyone looks super fancy with their brand-new outfits. I stay to myself in my little corner; I'm sort of shy at school. My only friends are Jane and a few other kids who sit at our lunch table, and the others are more acquaintances than real friends. About five minutes later, the other grades of students start to trickle in. You can tell they are older just based on their attitude; it's a lot more carefree.

But seriously, where *is* Jane? The doors should be opening any minute now. I check my phone for a response to my text, but there's still no reply.

I tap my foot nervously. All of a sudden, the loud chatter subsides.

The big doors unlock with a loud click, and students start entering the school. Somehow with all the pushing and squeezing, I go from all the way in the front of the crowd to the very back.

In the flood of people, I wave to my few other friends but continue desperately searching for Jane. Where is she? I hope she isn't going to be late; it's only the first day! That would be horrible—wait a second. Is that Jane? A small figure appears in the crowd, but my view is soon blocked by more people trying to enter.

I shuffle through the crowd to get a closer look. There she is again! Her familiar chestnut-brown hair flashes across my vision. Hold on; is she walking with the *popular kids*? I swear there are two blonde girls beside her! Or maybe not? I can't tell! More people attempt to push past me, obstructing my view of the girl I *think* is Jane.

Then, as quickly as the rush began, it ends, and I lose track of the supposed Jane. I blink a few times. It must have been my imagination. A few angry juniors ask me to move, and I hurry back to the corner. I probably shouldn't have been standing in the way, anyway.

I send a couple more texts. The clock continues to tick down to first period. At this point, everyone is in the building; I'm the only one left outside. A few people just arriving now give me quizzical looks as they enter the building. I look at my phone to avoid their eyes. Still no word from Jane.

Five more minutes pass. Only ten minutes left before the bell rings. I continue to anxiously check my texts. Nothing. Another five minutes go by. I'm really getting worried now. I have a silent debate with myself. Should I wait for Jane and risk being late, or do I go inside and have her think that I forgot about her? I bite my lip as I weigh the options. The warning bell breaks my train of thought, and I give in. I rush inside the building.

It takes me a few minutes to navigate through the halls, and I end up getting lost twice in the span of two minutes. I'm really cutting it close. I finally slip into my homeroom, and seconds later the bell rings. The teacher gives me an unhappy look, but dismisses my almost-tardiness. I sigh in relief.

It's probably not that big of a deal. Jane must have forgotten to meet me at the flagpole. It's typical for her to forget little details. But if she just forgot, then why didn't she reply to my text?

Other concerned questions cross my mind, but I push them away. Jane is probably fine! I'll see her in class and ask her what's up then, I decide.

The day drags on with a continuous cycle of listening to teachers drone on about expectations and then getting lost in the huge high-school hallways. I'm pretty distracted the first few periods—I keep wondering if Jane is okay. Maybe she was running late. After a few hours I sort of stop thinking about it.

I've been looking forward to one period more than any other: science. It's not so much that I like science, but Jane is in my class, so I'll actually have someone to talk to. And I can ask her about this morning. Did I mention Jane is super-duper, genius-level smart? She's in all advanced classes, and I'm pretty sure she is in college math. Science is my best subject, so I'm in Jane's "smart people" class this year.

I enter the room, quietly scanning the faces of everyone inside to find Jane. I perk up as I spot her familiar hair amid the swarm of people. At this point, I don't even care that she hasn't said hi to me yet; I'm just glad that she made it to school. I maneuver my way through the classroom and slide into an empty seat next to her. Jane is enthusiastically chatting with another girl I can't quite see. I tap her lightly on the shoulder, but she continues her conversation like nothing has happened.

"Jane!" I exclaim, trying to catch her attention. A cheery grin spreads across my face as she turns to look at me, but I am met with an unpleasant surprise.

The sight of her face catches me off guard. Her already clear skin is caked with layers of foundation and powder, and her eyelashes are coated in clumpy black mascara. She's wearing bright-pink lipstick, expertly applied. None of that really makes too much of a difference though; it's the expression on her face that really shocks me.

Jane looks disgusted with me. Her normally warm, friendly eyes are cold and judgmental, and her newly bright-pink lips are turned down in an annoyed scowl.

It's like I'm looking at a total stranger. Worst of all, her shift in orientation lets me see who she was talking to. It's Stacy Allen—the girl we've despised since elementary school. My third-grade bully! The only person we've ever really hated. But here's Jane, talking to her like they're best friends.

They are even wearing matching outfits. Jane always thought matching outfits were immature, but today she is wearing one with the fakest girl in school. Her skimpy jean shorts and tiny crop top makes my shin-length dress feel way too modest. "Confused" doesn't even begin to describe what I am feeling.

"Is there something you need?" she snaps. Stacy whispers into Jane's ear, and they both snicker loudly. I shake my head, my confusion apparent. They gather up their binders and move to two empty seats across the room from me. What is going on with Jane? In all the years I've known her, she has never acted like this.

The rest of the class is a nightmare. I torture myself thinking that I have done something wrong, that it's my fault Jane is acting totally different. Yesterday we were laughing and hanging out, just like we do every day. Now she doesn't even notice I am in the room, let alone *care*.

Lunch finally arrives, and I bring my tray to a lunch table in the middle of the cafeteria. It's normally me, Jane, and two of our other friends, but I can't find either of the others anywhere. I begin munching on my sandwich. School food isn't very good, but I can deal with their grilled cheeses every now and then. I look again for my other friends, but given that there are hardly any people left standing, they seem to have found another place to sit. I sigh sadly. I guess I'm eating lunch here. Alone.

It's so odd to eat lunch without Jane. I find myself longing for her company more than ever. I have so much to tell her about my day so far! She always loves hearing gossip about teachers and our fellow students. But from the looks of it, Jane doesn't want anything to do with me. I've seen her in a bad mood before, but this is different. It's not just her mood; it's like her entire personality changed overnight.

A few more minutes pass as I mindlessly chew my food and silently ponder my best friend's strange behavior. Then, all of a sudden, Jane comes up to me with her lunch.

She has a small smile on her face and waves at me. I look at her closely and see a spark of genuine happiness in her eyes. So she hasn't turned into a jerk—obviously! I knew she couldn't have changed so quickly. It must have been a prank. I always fall for her pranks! I just never knew that she was such a good actress. I guess the day isn't so horrible after all.

I return her smile and quickly invite her to sit next to me. She probably can't wait to tell me how gullible I am. After the confusion of the last few hours, I won't even mind if she does. Jane glances down at the chair I'm pointing to and puts her hand over her mouth. It looks like she is trying not to…laugh? A few seconds later, she bursts into uncontrollable laughter. Not "you fell for it!" laughter, but *mean* laughter.

My face falls as my eyes flicker across the room. I didn't even realize that Stacy and the rest of the popular girls are by her side, and they all are giggling along with her. I quickly push the chair back in, avoiding eye contact. I can feel their judgmental stares boring into the back of my head. Tears begin gathering in my eyes, but I refuse to let these girls see me cry. I keep my head down the whole time in embarrassment.

Jane momentarily pauses her snickering. She says a few words to her new friends and then leans in to whisper something in my ear. I want to cringe away, but I am frozen in place.

"Sorry, sweetie. I'm popular now; weirdos like you won't cut it anymore." Her fake-sweet voice almost hurts more than her words—it means this isn't a joke. My best friend really has turned against me.

Jane flips her hair and turns to leave, then pauses and decides against it. She walks back over to me and looks me up and down critically. I feel the need to cover myself from her eyes, but I still can't move. I try to open my mouth to ask her what is going on, but no words come out.

"And burn that hideous outfit.It looks like you picked it right out of the trash," she adds with another laugh. Her posse nods in agreement. Tears threaten to spill over as I look down at my blue dress in shame.

Jane doesn't notice my state of distress—or doesn't care—and blows me a fake kiss. She then gestures to the girls behind her and struts away with her new friends to a table across the cafeteria.

I am in pure shock. The tears I attempted to hold in cascade down my cheeks, and I hastily wipe them away with a rough napkin. It scratches my skin as I dab them away. She did not just say that. She did *not* just say that. All of a sudden my lunch doesn't seem very appetizing. I try to cover my tearstained face and red eyes from the passing students. I don't want anyone to think I'm a crybaby.

How can she have changed so much in less than twenty-four hours? It's like I'm not even talking to the same person! We were best friends just hours ago, and now…now she doesn't even care for me at all.

I can barely process what is happening. I dry the last few tears as more emotions overcome me.

I don't understand how all of this happened so quickly! What did I do to deserve this from her? After all of the years we've spent together—all of the memories that we've made together—she decides to throw it all away? Never in a million years would I have ever expected to be hurt by her. Jane is my best friend—no, she's like family to me.

This can't be happening. This can't be real. In one day, my best friend has destroyed thirteen years' worth of memories, and I don't think I'm ever going to get them back.

CHAPTER 1

"Come on! Turn left! I swear—no—ahhh!" I let out an angry shriek and hurl my headset across the room. It crashes against my wall with an epic thud, then falls meekly to the ground.

"Stupid game!" I mumble, vowing to never play it again. Who needs to play a weird video game about escaping a war, right? And yet, five minutes later, I pick the headset back up, plug it into the computer, and play again. And again. And again. And again and again and again. I'm addicted. I can't tear my eyes away from the screen for more than a minute without having a total freak-out. All I can think about is hitting that replay button over and over. The game is my escape. The more I play, the less time I have to acknowledge the growing knot of loneliness that is tightening in my stomach.

Freshman year was the worst year of my life. At the beginning of the year, I was constantly bullied by none other than my ex-best friend, and

I had no other friends to turn to—not a single one. So I stopped trying. I was the loner with no friends. I was no longer a straight-A student. I quit cross-country. I refused to talk about it to my parents, and I cut off my brother completely—I was alone. I gave up on everything. Why try to make new friends when the person you trusted most has left you? Why try to get good grades when you have someone constantly telling you that you're bad at everything? I didn't care that I was a failure; I just wanted to be invisible.

I turned to video games as a distraction. When I was playing, nothing else in the world mattered. It was a way to escape my terrible life. Every time I played, all of my worries faded into the background. I didn't need to think about anything.

It started as an hour a day. Then two hours. Then four hours. And so on until eventually it got to the point where I now spend every spare minute I have playing a video game. Not just any video game: *Escape the War*.

Escape the War is the best game to hit the market for decades. I guess people are drawn to the futuristic war-zone aspect of the game. It's centered around the concept of a war between humans and robots. You start out in the midst of the war zone, and you have to weave your way through the obstacles until you face the boss—but I've only ever gotten that far once. It's a little odd because there is only one really long level, but new updates hit almost every week, so it never gets boring!

I don't really know exactly what it is about the game, but I feel like I'm inside it when I play. I'm obsessed with it, and I'm not stopping anytime soon.

It starts out like a normal day for me: hopping onto my computer as soon as I can in order to get an early start. Now that it's summer, I can spend almost the entire day playing! After a number of minutes—or hours—pass, my door flings open and slams against my poor, defenseless desk. From the loud and overly aggressive way the door was opened, I can tell that it's my mom, and she is *not* happy.

"That's it. I'm done with your addiction! You haven't been out of your room in *days*, and all I hear you do is scream at that wretched game!" She pauses, glaring at me, although my attention is directed at the screen. I let out a small exclamation of anger as my character is destroyed by an obstacle. I was close that time! "Are you even listening to me?" my mother bellows, stomping her foot on the floor.

"One second!" I mumble, keeping my eyes glued to the game. My mom lets out an exasperated sigh, clearly trying to control her furious emotions. I feel her anger turn to disappointment as she stares at me. I pretend not to notice.

"Look at yourself! What happened to you?" she says quietly. Inside, I pause to think the same thing, but I refuse to let her know that she is right. Instead, I act like I didn't hear her. Her disappointment immediately turns back into fury. She takes a deep breath and exits my room, giving the door a colossal yank to close it. It sounds about ready to break off the hinges.

Maybe she's right. I pause the game and glance at myself in the mirror. My wavy brown hair is greasy and unbrushed, and my hazel eyes look tired. I stare at my sickly pale skin, remembering when I had a tan at all times from spending all day outside. My bony figure is hunched over in my chair, exposing my scrawny arms. I look away from the mirror, thinking over what my mom said.

My eyes flick over to the large piece of paper draped over the bulletin board right above me. I tear off the paper covering and stare at it blankly.

It's a collage of all of my best memories with my friends. Picture after picture of me smiling, laughing, and having a blast. Insecurity washes over me as I eye my past self's tan skin and beautiful brown locks. I feel a tinge of jealousy for my once-perfect life. *What* did *happen to me?*

My gaze wanders to the people next to me in each photo, and I cringe away. Almost every photo was taken with Jane. Her happy grin and our silly faces haunt me. With every picture I see, the knot in my stomach tightens more.

Our smiling faces at the beach. Tighter. Laughing together at my birthday party. Tighter. Us ziplining together. Even tighter. I skim the rest of the pictures, welling up as the pain of my loneliness overtakes me.

Just as I am about to break down in tears, the urge to play the game takes me over once again. I yank the bulletin board from the wall and hurl it into my closet. I fling myself back into the game with a completely different mindset.

Ugh. What was I even thinking about? Who cares about friends when I have *Escape the War*? It is hands-down the best game on the planet. In fact, it's *better* than real life. I wish I lived in *Escape the War*. I wouldn't have to worry about *anything!* No parents. No stupid siblings. And best of all, no horrible people who pretend to be your friend and then snap your friendship in half like it was worth nothing. And just like that, I convince myself that my moment of regret was nothing but a small lapse of judgment.

Several frustrating runs later, I venture into the "store" to buy some extra gems and something catches my eye. There's a new special pack with the oddest description—it claims that you can "live the game." I assume it's a ticket to the sort of live-action choose-your-own-adventure games you find at sports complexes. I look up the address on my cell phone. A five-star rating—this place must be legit! It might be nice to get out of the house for a little while, too. I'll still be playing the game, but I'll be doing it while I'm out and about.

I shuffle through my desk until I find the scratched-up gift card I got for my birthday last month and enter the information so the transaction can be made. I yawn, tapping my fingers lightly on my chair as a distraction. It's taking a lot longer than online purchases normally do. Oddly enough, I feel my eyes getting heavier and heavier by the second. It's getting harder to keep them open. I don't think that I've realized how tired I am until now. Now that I think about it, I don't think I remember the last time I slept, either. A little nap can't hurt, right? The world seems to blur. My eyes droop shut, and I fall into a shallow doze.

I wake up with a start. I'm falling! I'm falling down a sort of tube. But I was just in my room! *Am I dreaming?* I wonder as I plummet down the seemingly endless shaft. In the blur of the moment, I manage to pinch myself. The realization hits me: I am wide awake. I let out a startled yelp, which grows into a horrified scream. The last thing I remember is buying that pack from the store in the game in my room. How did I get here from there? And where *is* here?

The tube is very narrow, and it's pitch black. The only thing I can see is a speck of light down below, growing closer by the second. Oh my gosh, am I going to die? I scream louder and flail my arms and legs around desperately in the small space, praying I find something to grab onto.

The other end of the tube is getting closer, and I have no way to slow my fall. I'm mere feet away now. This is it—this is how I die. I brace myself as I finally reach the circle of light.

I land on a hard surface with a gigantic thud. It feels as if every bone in my body has snapped in half. I'm in so much pain that I can't even process where I am. All I can hear is indistinct voices murmuring about my "arrival." A short, fit girl carefully strides towards me and proceeds to hoist me on her back like I weigh nothing.

"Stop. Let me go," I mutter weakly, flailing my arms. I throw a weak punch at her face, which she avoids by simply tilting her head to the side. Am I being *kidnapped*?

"Ada, don't scare the kid!" a kind voice commands.

"Sorry, Sawyer! She hit *pre-tty* hard, and I don't think she can walk," Ada replies. She sets me down on a relatively comfortable sofa as several more strangers surround me. I'm practically blinded by pain at the moment, but I can feel tension in the room, as if these people are constantly on guard. My intense pain is still throbbing, but it's subsiding much more quickly than I thought it would. I guess I didn't break any bones. Once I've gained back enough of my strength, I sit up. I have absolutely no idea what's going on or why five people are staring at me.

I glance down and find myself in black skinny jeans and a camo tank top, and my jaw practically falls open. I was just wearing sweats—when did I change? Did *someone else* change my clothes? I am accumulating questions by the second.

"Wh- where am I? Who are you?" I ask, eyeing the strangers warily. I try not to sound too hostile in case I really *was* kidnapped. I don't want to make them mad and get killed. And I can't help but feel like I already know these people. There's something familiar about them that I just can't place.

A gorgeous blonde lady standing across from us in a closed-off area groans loudly when her watch starts beeping. She looks familiar too! The woman nudges the man next to her, then exits the area to stand inside a small glass cubicle. The floor drops out from under her, and she disappears into a black tube. The screen to my right flashes on. It's showing a play-through from *Escape the War*—and that blonde lady is in it!

"W- what? How is she…?!" I stammer. More questions pile into my brain and I want to scream.

"Can someone please tell me what the heck is going on?" I shout, finally throwing my self-control out the window. The strangers seem surprised at my outburst and one of them almost laughs. I glare at them. This isn't funny! They all look towards one person.

A middle-aged man with gray streaks in his long, dirty-blond hair sits down next to me. He sighs quietly, takes a deep breath, and begins to explain.

"Welcome to homebase. You're probably really into *Escape the War*—like *obsessed* into it, am I right?" the man begins. I nod sheepishly, not happy to admit to my addiction in front of a bunch of strangers. Why does that even matter?

"So, one day, a 'special pack' that lets you 'live the game' suddenly pops up in the store, and you buy it," he continues. I nod again. How does he know that?

"Well...the pack worked. You have been transported inside the game," the man states flatly. I stare at him. Okay, *what?!*

"Now you get to 'live the game.' Literally. You are now one of the characters a player can select whenever he or she decides to play. That means you get to endure everything that the characters you used to play had to. We all look familiar, right? That's because *we* are the characters that *you* have been playing the past few weeks."

I blink in shock, waiting for the memories to resurface. The images of the characters in the game's menu swarm my mind, each face lining up with one in front of me. I knew they looked familiar! But how is that possible?

"There are two shifts of players to allow for adequate rest for both shifts. You are first shift. The player's character options change each shift, so there will be no 'Ivy' available for the second half of the day. The watch you have on your wrist beeps whenever a player wants to play as you."

I glance down at my wrist to see a petite white watch there. I yank as hard as I can in an attempt to remove it, but I have no luck.

"Don't bother. It won't come off. Unfortunately, living in this game…it's not temporary. I've been stuck in this nightmarish game for twenty-five years. There is no escape. Only the same thing. Over and over and *over.*"

His head lowers sadly. My expression is impassive. My brain is whizzing to try and comprehend the situation, but I just *can't.* How am I supposed to accept the fact that someone told me I was transferred into a *video game*? A *video game*!

Despite my own feelings of panic and confusion, I notice that the man looks hopeless. The sad part is, I can see the ghost of who he used to be. It's hidden deep inside him, but behind those dull eyes, I see a man who used to have ambitions. Under all of that misery, I feel like he could have been such a humorous person—nothing like the mask his hopelessness has put on him. Maybe not; maybe he would have been shy, or optimistic, or patient! That's just the thing—I don't know. Whatever personality Crosby used to have has been buried under all of his sorrow, and it only is revealed in small pieces, practically impossible to see. It's not only him, but everyone else too. I'm not sure what happened, but these people have been broken.

I shake my head vigorously. Did I really start to believe them for a moment there? I bet these people are just a bunch of older teenagers trying to prank me. I narrow my eyes at each person, carefully examining them. They must be some pretty good actors.

I glance at the buff guy in the corner. *He definitely looks like someone from my school*, I think. Even if he isn't, I've figured it out—Jane probably set this up to humiliate me. It must have been hard for her to find people who look enough like the characters from *Escape the War*. Or maybe I'm supposed to believe the characters were modeled after them—ha!

My blank expression becomes a smile, and I burst out laughing. The people around me immediately become alarmed. They're looking at me like

I have three heads, but I just can't stop. I laugh and laugh until my abs hurt and I can barely breathe. Between giggles, I manage to spit out a few words.

"That was a good one—you almost got me!" I exclaim, patting one of them on the back. She glares at me and stiffly brushes my hand off her back. It's the same lady who first picked me up when I arrived here—Ada, I think. At least that was her name in *Escape the War*.

The woman stands still, staring at me. She almost looks…*angry*. Her body tenses up, and a fire lights in her eyes. My laughter halts abruptly. She snickers sarcastically, then mumbles some rude remarks under her breath. She's getting mad, and fast. Uh-oh.

What did I do?

She briskly leaves the area. The others break into quiet chatter, speculating about what she is about to do. I just stand there. Waiting.

The lady emerges from a room seconds later with a large billboard-looking object in her hands. She strides towards me and slams it on the ground in front of me. I wince, then curiously open one eye to see what it is.

It seems to be made from…napkins. The small white squares are lined up and layered precisely.

Metal paper clips connect the napkins, creating a billboard-like appearance. As Ada carries the large object, the swaying napkins allow me to get a sneak peek of what she is trying to show me. Through the small gaps, I spot pencil marks on the front of each square. I squint my eyes and attempt to scoot closer for a better view. I don't understand—why is Ada showing me random lines on some napkins?

She sees my confusion and turns it around, revealing hundreds of tally marks lined up in rows. The early rows are neatly drawn, with little encouraging messages that gradually become less enthusiastic. As the tallies go on, the marks become sloppier and sloppier and the motivational messages disappear altogether. Hundreds of tallies later, there is a series of pencil-holes in the makeshift board. I am quiet. I don't need anyone to tell me what this means, what all of this means.

It's keeping track of the number of days she has been here. She slowly lost hope until she eventually…gave up. Despite myself, I realize I am actually starting to believe them. The lady points to the large array of pencil-stabbed holes at the bottom of the napkin-board.

"That was exactly one year ago. Now does this seem like a joke?"

My face falls as the realization thuds into my brain like a ton of bricks. Even though I've been told multiple times, this is when it actually sinks in. My wish came true.

I'm inside *Escape the War.*

CHAPTER 2

The same man who explained about the game reaches out his hand. I eye him hesitantly before placing my own hand out.

"Crosby Dame," he says gruffly. I shake his hand.

"Ivy Judinson," I say in a low voice. The other four people say goodbye and slowly begin to disperse. I sneak a glance at each person to see who I might want to be friends with. They don't seem to be *that* bad; I think I can manage. Besides, it's been so long since I've had a friend. It might be nice to try again.

Crosby clears his throat to regain my attention, then motions for me to follow him. I finally get to observe my surroundings! I realize I'm in living quarters of some sort. This must be the "house" area that the players live in when they aren't on their shift. The place I landed seems to be a common-room area, furnished with several chairs and a table along with a wide screen. A large chute runs from the ceiling to just above the table. In one corner there's an odd glass enclosure, which is separated into small wood-paneled cubicles.

I move closer to the sectioned-off area. Above each cubicle is a large screen displaying a character description. I examine the first screen and gasp at what I read there.

Corinne

Strengths	**Weaknesses**
+5 Stealth	-5 Strength
+10 Smarts	-10 Speed
+15 Endurance	

Weapon: Throwing Knives

Bonus! Unlock a special accessory!

It's my favorite player. I've had Corinne's basic stats memorized for months; she was one of the only players I ever used. A twinge of guilt strikes me as I think of how many runs I have taken with her. I can't believe that this whole time, I was making a real person do that. I scan the row of screens to find the same statistics that I've seen in the character selection menu so many times. The faces—oh, they all look so familiar!

I played less often late in the day, when the second shift was active, but when I did, I used Ada—the short girl with the whole napkin situation—the most. Despite the striking resemblance and identical name, I couldn't bring myself to admit that this girl could really be Ada until now. The guilt grows stronger. I can't believe myself. Although I only vaguely remember playing as other second-shift people, their faces are familiar too.

"It's weird, huh?" Crosby comments from behind me. I nod and take one last look before I turn to follow him. We head through a narrow hallway lined with ten identical doors until we reach one near the end of it.

He opens the door into a small room with a twin-sized bed, a table, and grey walls. It's quite bland—they could've at least used a pop of yellow or something. Seems like these people could use a little brightness in their lives.

"This will be your room," he says flatly. I walk over to the bed and run my hand across the sheets.

"Is that it?" I ask Crosby. He shakes his head, signifying that he has more to show me. I follow him back through the hallway until we reach a small room.

It's even tinier than my bedroom, but a doorway at the back leads to a larger room lined with glass-fronted cabinets. I move closer and squint to see through the glass. There are so many clothes and accessories through that door—it must be the wardrobe from the game's character customization menu. That's where you can accessorize your character with all sorts of cool items. I'm ecstatic! After seeing my bedroom, I figured that all aspects of life here would be bland and boring, but at least we get to choose our outfits. Through the glass, I eye a gorgeous necklace that I absolutely love and a few tops that would look so cute with it. Hundreds of combinations cross my mind as I survey the room, and I only become more and more excited. Fashion was one of my passions before I got addicted to *Escape the War*; maybe I can finally get back to pursuing it! This could be my chance.

I speed-walk up to the door and am enthusiastically reaching for the doorknob when Crosby harshly grabs my wrist.

"You do *not* change an outfit unless your wristwatch tells you to, do you hear me? You can't just do whatever you want!" I wince and withdraw my hand immediately, but something flickers in my memory. That phrase is so familiar—not in Crosby's harsh tone, but I have definitely heard those exact words before. Not from just anyone, but from my dad.

It was the peak of summer, and my four-year-old self was bouncing along Bronco Lane hand-in-hand with my best friend, Jane. We trailed behind my dad, who was chuckling silently at our loud conversations about the most random things. We skipped around the block, laughing, smiling and having the best time ever.

We had no worries in the world; enjoying each other's company was our only thought. Our feet padded down the sidewalk in sync as we admired the beautiful flora blooming around us.

"Daddy, wait!" I exclaimed. My dad came to an abrupt halt and turned to face us. I leaned forward on my tip-toes and stretched my arm as far as I could. After a couple tries, I managed to grab two small flowers from a tree. With a big smile, I tucked one behind my ear and placed one behind Jane's at the same time. We exchanged happy glances.

"Come on, girls," my dad said, amused. Jane and I rushed to catch up with him. When we turned the corner, we came face to face with the biggest candy shop we had ever seen.

Jane ran to the window at the front to gawk at the sweets on display. I hurriedly joined her, leaving my dad far behind us. My eyes lit up at the sight of the hundreds of colorful candies in different shapes and sizes. I bounced up and down at the sight of our favorite lollipop, my pointer finger shooting out to direct my father's attention to it. Jane also grinned from ear to ear at the sight of our favorite treat, and she joined me in my pleas to my father.

After a few seconds, he finally caught up to us and glanced upwards to the window before shaking his head. He made eye contact with me and then Jane before wagging his finger at us. Then, he grabbed our hands and continued walking. Jane slumped over sadly, but gave in after a few tugs and started walking.

I stayed right where I was, my hand stuck in its position. My dad looked at me, more sternly now, and firmly mouthed the word "no."

My smile turned into a frown, and tears started falling. Jane was getting upset now too. I intensified my sobbing (I was definitely causing a scene) but my father would not budge. I got louder and louder, but my dad ignored my pleas, and instead calmed Jane down to prevent more of a crying mess.

No matter how many times he said no, I refused to stop crying. So my dad sat on a nearby bench and waited.

  Jane, upset that I was still crying, took it upon herself to make me stop. Her calming nature in itself calmed me a bit, but didn't stop the waterworks.

  "Ivy, I know what will make you feel better!" Jane said brightly. I paused my tears and glanced upwards. There stood Jane, all smiles, with her hand extended out in a ready position. Even through my tears, I managed to crack a tiny smile.

  "Up! Down! Left and right! Together we will be all right!" Our small hands moved together perfectly, and by the end of our secret handshake, I wasn't crying anymore.

  "Told you! Now come on, we have the whole town to walk through," Jane added with a grin. She removed the plucked magnolia from her hair and delicately placed it in mine. I smiled gratefully. My dad stared at us in wonder, and kneeled down to face me eye-to-eye.

  "Ivy, darling, Jane's right. You can't just do whatever you want! That's not how life works. Now come on, let's go have some fun!" He gently wiped away my remaining tears and gave me a big squeeze. Jane hooked her arm around mine, and we skipped off as if nothing had happened.

  "Ivy? Ivy?" I snap out of my daydream, nodding to signal I've come back to the present moment.

I guess I won't be having fun coming up with outfits. Crosby continues, "You have a one-hour break until we must report to our assigned sectors." He leads me out of the wardrobe and points to the big black clock in the living room that's slowly counting down.

"Now, there's one more thing I need to show you." His expression, already unhappy, turns to stone-cold anger. Oh, crap. What did I do now?

Crosby spots my terrified reaction and softens his hard expression.

"It's not you; I'm just not very fond of this part of protocol," he says with a grimace. As if I weren't confused enough already… Before I can bombard him with more questions, he gestures for me to follow him.

CHAPTER 3

We end up in a small, musty room at the corner of the living quarters. An old-timey TV rests on a table in the back, and a dusty recliner sits opposite to the television. Crosby walks over to the TV and slides a small circular disc into the box positioned under the TV.

"Is that…a DVD player? The last time I saw one of those was in my dad's antique collection!" I scoff and crack a genuine smile for the first time since I arrived here. He eyes me, unamused.

"We aren't exactly getting shipments of the latest technology," he snaps. My smile fades. I had just wanted to lighten the mood! After Crosby fiddles with the buttons for a few moments, colors begin to rapidly appear on the screen, forming the title: "The Origin of *Escape the War*."

"Ohhh! I get it, this is like a history lesson! But why would— " Crosby stops me mid-sentence and gestures to the TV. It's starting. A small, mousy woman with curly blonde hair appears on the screen. Her face is devoid of any imperfections and her movements are strangely robotic.

"Is she a— " I start curiously.

"Will you *please* shut up for five minutes and watch the stupid video?" he interrupts, clearly annoyed. I huff, but decide to stop with the unwelcome questions for now.

"Welcome to *Escape the War*. Please enjoy our short summary of the history of this game."

Her voice is the sort of cloyingly fake-sweet that sounds like nails on a chalkboard. It makes me shudder.

"It all started thirty years ago, in 2007! Our amazing and talented CEO, the GameMaster, decided to create a brand-new video game!" Crosby scoffs at the compliments, and I suppress a gag. This lady's voice is *way! too! enthusiastic!* for my taste.

A picture of a hooded figure flashes on the screen. I attempt to catch a glimpse of the figure's face, but it's completely obscured.

"She wanted the game to have a war zone–inspired setting with a post-apocalyptic aesthetic. Inspired by the concept of a robot vs. human battle, she combined the three elements in perfect balance, and *Escape the War* was born! The GameMaster, previously a programmer, used research on the psychology of video games to formulate an engaging plot (that keeps people intrigued) and an exciting situation (that makes *everyone* want to play)!" I suck in a breath. A developer really made me that addicted to a game with *research*?

"Those are two parts of *Escape the War*'s success, but the GameMaster is the world's best programmer! She wanted to make sure people *never lose interest.* Every other developer was just using a few psychological techniques to keep people playing, but the GameMaster combined hundreds of small existing mind games with techniques she invented herself! That perfect combination causes the brains of players to become a *tad* more invested than usual. For example, *Escape the War*'s instantaneous replay option lets players try again—just one more time—with one small click, and the 'easy to learn, tough to master' mindset makes players believe they understand the game perfectly, they just need to practice—play—more. After all, practice makes perfect!" she finishes with a cheery grin. That is *sick*.

"The game was a huge success! It even became one of the top ten most popular games in the world! But of course, overachiever that she is, the GameMaster thought the game needed more… realism! The inclusion of real people in the game would give the player a sensation of 'being there' unlike anything they've ever felt while playing a video game, setting her game apart from anything else on the market!" I shiver at her still-joyful attitude. A thought crosses my mind. When I played the game, I experienced that sensation—and that's why I couldn't stop. As much as I hate to say it, whatever she did worked. But that doesn't make it any less horrible.

"A few specific players of our game had unfortunate events going on in their lives. Those players of the game were the most invested in *Escape the War*. That's how we began to find candidates for our characters! The more 'into' the game someone is, the better chance they have for becoming a character!" she exclaims, fake excitement filling her voice. I feel my cheeks flush with anger at the thought of Jane's abandonment and my retreat into the game afterwards. She's responsible for getting me into this mess too?

"With the help of her team of programmers, the GameMaster managed to transfer humans with the most investment in the game *inside*

Escape the War! And you are one of them! Thanks to your help, the game has a sense of realism that is found in no other game in the world! You might ask, *Why would she do this?* Well, the GameMaster is number one in everything she does. She never loses. She is the smartest and most innovative programmer of the century! Why would her game be any different? She wanted the game to reflect her as a person; the GameMaster wanted *Escape the War* to be the best." A few screenshots from inside the game appear momentarily on the screen.

I'm disgusted. This is all about her stupid ego?

"The GameMaster's determination to be the best has made *Escape the War* the number-one highest-grossing game for twenty-five years!" Headlines about the game's success fill the screen, almost covering the mousy-robot lady.

"We thank you for your service and hope you enjoy your time in *Escape the War*." The screen turns black.

"'And we hope you enjoy your time in *Escape the War*,'" I mimic furiously. "What is this, a hotel?" To my surprise, Crosby lets out a small chuckle. He shakes his head and switches off the TV. A thought crosses my mind, and after a few moments of hesitation, I give it a go.

"Hey, you know how she said that the characters for the game had uh—you know, like, unfortunate events going on in, um, their lives?" I stammer. He raises his eyebrows. "What happened? You know, to you? Like, to get you—"

"Get me trapped inside the game?" he finishes for me. I nod sheepishly. I definitely shouldn't have asked, but it might make me feel a little better to know that I'm not the only one with emotional trauma, however messed up that may sound. I just want to know that I'll have someone to understand me, although I'm not sure Crosby would have been my first choice.

"You know, you're the first person to ever ask me that straight out," he responds honestly. I flinch. That can't be good. "Actually, it's a good thing. That way, I can teach you what not to do instead of letting you learn the hard way." I grimace. So I was right.

"Game origin stories—that's what you just described. How you got addicted and trapped inside this game. It's something we all have but never want to talk about. The one thing that we do everything possible to avoid discussing. Those points in our lives were the lowest points that we've ever had to go through. We'd be lying if we said that we didn't want to forget them, and I'm sure you relate to that as well." I cringe a little, but agree. "That means you don't just go around asking people for them; eventually, they'll share it with you if they're ready," Crosby explains. I nod. I guess that makes sense. I'd be pretty upset if someone straight-up asked me about Jane and our friendship break-up, but still. It would be nice to have someone to relate to.

It looks like Crosby is debating something silently, but I'm standing there awkwardly wondering if we are going to go back into the hallway or not. After a little more weird silence, I can't take it anymore.

"So are we going to go back out there, or—" I begin.

"Oh, why not?" Crosby exclaims, cutting me off. I'm confused; is he talking about going back to the common area?

"I'm sorry?" I ask. He waves his hand dismissively.

"You were the only one brave enough to ask about my past, so why not give it to you?" I want to tell him that wasn't bravery, it was fear of being alone, but he talks too quickly. "My story is a little more unique than the others'. Most of them only found and used *Escape the War* as a way to deal with their emotions, but for me it was different." I blush slightly—I guess I'm really not the only one.

"*Escape the War* had been my favorite game since I was five or six. I loved it! But I didn't have a major addiction, just a small one." I nod. That makes sense. That's probably how *Escape the War* feels to a normal player: just a really fun, slightly addicting game.

"I think I was a little younger than you when it happened; twelve, maybe? My parents both worked in the same office, and one day, there was this freak fire. It killed them both. One minute I was a normal middle-schooler, and the next day I was an orphan." Crosby's expression is blank. If I were discussing something as terrible as this, tears would be streaming down my face, but he looks unbothered. Somehow I get the feeling that he wasn't always this matter-of-fact about it.

"*Escape the War* was like my comfort object. It was the only thing that I could go back to that reminded me of my old life. From orphanage to orphanage, I held onto that game, playing it on any console I could find. I hoped to regain some of the happiness of my old life. I never did. But my frustration translated into more playing. It went way beyond the casual interest I had in it before—it became an obsession. And then you know what happened: I got addicted, blah blah blah, and I ended up here." I struggle to find something to say. How am I supposed to reply to that?

"No need to comment if you don't want to. Now, let's get you back to your room!" Crosby says.

CHAPTER 4

The walk back to my room is silent. I can't help but think about how terrible Crosby's origin story is. That poor man! Are the others' pasts just as bad? And even worse, that cruel woman that put us all in here all for the sake of her inflated ego. She wanted to be the best so badly that she destroyed our lives to make it happen. How can she live with that? If only we could figure out who she is! Although I guess it wouldn't make a difference—we can't do much to take her down from here.

We soon reach my room, and Crosby leaves after saying a quick farewell (but not before reminding me that my first shift starts in an hour). I sit on the bed for a little while, examining my surroundings. There isn't much, only the necessities. A white dresser sits in the corner of the room. I open one of the drawers, but unsurprisingly, it's empty. The bedding is also white, reminding me of a hotel's. The sheets are soft, comfortable, clean—everything you could ask for—but they aren't the ones at home. I suddenly find myself missing my scratchy old blue bedding.

The bedside table is made from a light-colored wood that matches the bed frame. On it sits a large book. I rush to open it, hoping it's one of the classics, a piece of my childhood that I can keep beside me at night. My hopes are quickly smashed; it's a rule manual. I sigh sadly and reach over to place it back on the table, then pause. Maybe it could actually be kind of helpful. I shake my head and chuckle at myself—it's a boring rule manual! As soon as I put it back down, I sit quietly on my bed, looking for something to do. And then I realize there *is* nothing to do. With a groan, I pick up the book again and stare at its bland cover with reluctance.

Am I really going to be someone who reads this type of stuff for fun? Well…I don't get what's happening here, so reading it can't do any harm. I slide into the cool covers and pry open the gigantic tome. I read the first few pages eagerly, but soon I fall into a bored daze. This is worse than reading the textbooks at school. It isn't very good for a distraction, or even for helping me understand what is going on. My mind drifts to other topics much heavier on my mind.

What is my mom thinking right now? Did she call the police? Does she think I ran away? What if she thinks I'm *dead*? Even though I don't exactly have the best relationship with them right now, I can't stand the idea of my mom—my dad—Chad—thinking I am dead. I fling off the pristine white sheets and sprint out of my room. Of course, with my luck, I slam into Crosby by accident. He heaves an angry sigh and turns around to face me.

"Well?" he asks, clearly frustrated with me. I cringe away before remembering my burning questions.

"Um…what will my parents think? Will they think I'm dead? Will they think I ran away? What about my brother? Will he—" Crosby cuts off my flood of questions with a gesture.

"Please—relax! Your family and friends will simply think you've gone missing, it's not a big deal." My eyes widen. *Not a big deal?* This is a *really* big deal! Crosby sees my frantic expression and face-palms.

I pause and take a deep breath to calm myself down. I haven't been talking to my family much lately, but that doesn't mean that I'm okay with them thinking I've gone missing, but Crosby is right. There's nothing I can do from here, and freaking out is not going to help.

As I slowly walk back to my room, I peek through each cracked-open door to see what the others are doing. A few are writing or drawing. One person is even playing an instrument! Where did they get this stuff? All of my drawers were completely empty!

"We make them," Crosby says quietly from behind me. I jump in surprise.

"Oh. Okay," I reply, my cheeks turning red. I sneak back into my room and shut the door.

Make them? How do you make an instrument from nothing but old household materials? I collapse on the bed. I don't know how I'm going to do this for the next few hours, let alone the rest of my life!

Maybe it's just a dream?

I pray that last thought is true as I drift into sleep. Too soon, my watch starts beeping loudly. I wake in a state of panic, not knowing where I am, but I slump over sadly when I realize I'm still in the same place.

Wait a second—my shift!

I jump up and scramble out of my room, unsure whether or not I need any materials for my shift. I'm supposed to be in my sector by now! I race through the empty hallway. Once I reach the common area, I see a row of small sliding doors closing quickly. The people I saw when I first arrived are already inside. I hurry towards the last empty cubicle and scramble under the sliding door, nearly strangling myself in the process. I'm standing there, out of breath, when my stats flash on the screen above me.

Ivy

Strengths	**Weaknesses**
+5 Precision	-5 Weapon Skill
+5 Agility	-5 Strength
·15 Speed	

Weapon: Coming Soon

Bonus! New character!

I scoff. I'm not that weak! I guess I am pretty fast. Or at least I used to be, back before I quit cross-country. I could probably get back to my old nimble self if I really want to. That's the thing about the stats of each character: they are never set in stone. Every week, they are constantly revolving to highlight the new strengths and weaknesses of each character. Some stats almost never change—like Crosby's—while others change on a weekly basis—like Ada's. I used to think that they were all just randomly generated, but now I know that they actually depend on how we do on our runs. No pressure there.

My watch jerks me from my self-analysis. I turn around to find that it's the only one beeping.

The sliding door immediately begins to open again—apparently I sprinted here for no reason. A few crudely drawn arrows on the ground point towards the glass enclosure, which also has an open door.

A familiar-ish man yells directions and information from inside his wooden cubicle. I learn that the black hole in the floor of the glassed-in area is the "run tube"—that's how you get into the world of the game. You can only go when your watch beeps to indicate that a player has chosen you.

I'm about to play as a character inside the game for the first time.

I follow the arrows into the glass enclosure and stand anxiously by the run tube. The beeping of my watch subsides, and its white screen is replaced by a black countdown clock like the one in the living room. It begins to count down from ten.

"The first run is the hardest. It will get better, I promise!" the man shouts encouragingly. I grimace, but I try to look grateful. At least someone is attempting to be nice to me. The clock continues to count down, and I shake off my nerves as best as I can. There's no point in worrying. After all, it's just a video game. It can't be that bad, right?

There's only one way to find out. When it hits one second left to go, I hurl myself into the black tube without a second thought.

It's like going down one of the tube slides from the elementary-school playground—the one that everyone crowds around during recess, impatient for a turn. Except I don't get to enjoy the rush of exhilaration and memories that come at me because I am so nervous about what is waiting at the *end* of the tube. Seconds later, I land on a stone pathway and barely catch myself before I fall flat on my face. I brush the dirt from my pants and look up.

I'm overwhelmed by what I see.

I'm in a completely different setting—yet it is so familiar. I am in the war zone where the game starts. The only difference? I'm so used to seeing this world from my computer screen that I never thought about how scary it would be from an inside view.

The pathway I'm standing on is made of cracked cobblestone, and it's spattered with bloodstains. A shiver goes through my spine. Several feet ahead of me is a group of menacing robots with huge rifles, all pointed at me. I jump back in fear, but they remain still. Of course—my run hasn't actually started yet. They are dressed in torn-up soldiers' uniforms and are all staring at me threateningly. I can't quite get over their cold, lifeless stares.

Before the first group of robots is a fork in the path with a series of deadly bombs lined up right at the split. They look ready to explode the moment I come near them.

Up ahead, I eye a couple of floating robots with laser guns, prepared to hit me with their perfect aim. Their blocky metal torsos hover above me, watching my every move. I shiver again. The worst part about these robots is that they are always perfect. They never miss. They don't make mistakes. Because they aren't human.

Of all the many variations of robots, the flying ones are the worst. All of the robots in the game have the same clunky, rusted quality—like they've been built from junkyard scraps—but each different type has one unique aspect. Some of them can recover their "health" quickly, others are incredibly speedy, and a few can even teleport. They are grouped together by "special feature" and are placed throughout the game accordingly. They're all pretty terrifying, but it's especially scary to know that a deadly robot is flying right above your head and there's nothing you can do about it.

I can't see any farther up ahead from here, but from my past playing experience, I know that there are at least five more groups of robots with special powers—and that's just until I get to the guards at the military base. As a player goes further and further into the game, the special powers of the robots increase, making the robots become more deadly—and I have to defeat them. All of them.

It's not like once I defeat one group of robots I won't have to do it again, either. The game is basically one really long level, with only a few placemarkers to save your progress: one after you get past the bombs at the fork in the road, one right before you get to the final group of robots (the teleporters!), and one when you get past the guards to the military outpost. These save points are pretty far apart, so I'll be fighting the same bots for many runs. The progress-saving spots aren't even very helpful. The game updates weekly, continually adding new obstacles and replacing old ones; each update resets all of your progress. I remember this being awfully frustrating, but still, it was one of the many things that made me want to constantly play *Escape the War*: it's a race against time.

The sky is a dark copper with grey smoke obscuring anything else that might be nearby. It's not like there's only a little farther ahead, either. I know that the battlefield goes on for at least a couple of miles, filled to the brim with challenges. Small airplanes litter the sky, ready to drop missiles at any moment. The sounds of war are growing louder and more intense.

Worst of all, I'm standing on a sort of wide bridge. I peek over the edge to find a thousand-foot drop into a dry, barren wasteland. I gulp. I don't remember the drop seeming so high from the player's perspective.

Everything about this is just…terrifying. As if the peril-filled landscape weren't scaring me enough, the hyper-realistic graphics that render it are definitely not helping. I could probably deal with it if the game's graphics were cartoony, but of course, The GameMaster just *had* to make this the most realistic game possible. Every detail is perfectly programmed to look exactly like real life. Even the one loose stone on the ground is perfectly shaded in all of the right places.

It's not only the frightening scenery that's bothering me. Sure, that's part of it, but I feel odd. Very odd. It's like…I'm not in control of what I'm doing. Then it hits me. I knew I'd be a character inside the game—but I didn't realize that the player would be *controlling* me!

I should have known. When you play the game, you see everything from your character's perspective. The player *is* the character during the runs. Still, I can't help but be shocked at how strange it feels to not have command of my own body.

It reminds me of what I've read about sleep paralysis, which is when you are conscious and completely aware of everything that is going on, but trapped inside your own skin. The difference—and the scariest part—is that not only am I trapped, but someone else is moving my body for me. Sure, I can think for myself, but my thoughts have no power over what I'm actually doing. My limbs feel numb, as if they have been disconnected from my body.

It's the most helpless I've ever felt in my life.

A loud, booming voice jolts me from my thoughts, but my body remains motionless. Of course, the introduction to the game! As the voice speaks, a gigantic screen (clearly a large hologram) covers my view of the war zone, and large white text appears on it to accompany the narration.

"The year is 2300. Almost a decade ago, a terrible mistake in an experiment with artificial intelligence created a class of power-hungry, autonomous robots. These robots vowed to end humanity for good, causing a great war between the two species. Unfortunately, their promise has almost come true. The war between our two species has been raging on for years, but humans are on the verge of extinction. Our population is dwindling, we are running out of supplies, and our battle tactics are easily outmatched by the opposing side's. The robots won't stop until every human being is dead." I can't tell where the voice is coming from! I attempt to swivel my head to get a better idea, but I am frozen in place. I already forgot that I'm controlled by the player, and it's barely been a minute. The voice commands my attention once more, its monotonous tone persistent.

"General Kerrigan, our commander, has chosen you to undertake the mission that is humanity's last chance. Fight your way inside the fortress of the robots' leader, Cybel, and destroy him and all of his minions. This will put an end to the war and secure a future for mankind. There will be many obstacles along the way, but if you do not succeed, we face the extinction of our species. There is no more time left, no more options. Good luck, and remember, you are our last hope to escape the war." The speaker's voice fades into nothing as the screen disintegrates as fast as it appeared. I gulp nervously. I've played this game more than enough times to know that it's *really scary*. I can't imagine what the rest of these bots are going to look like in person!

My watch beeps again and begins a countdown from five. My immediate reaction is to freak out. When the clock hits zero, am I supposed to run? Do I wait for the player to tell me what to do? How do I know where to run? My panic only rises as the clock gets closer and closer to zero. All of a sudden, a small handgun appears in my right hand. The words "default weapon" are plastered on the weapon. I don't know how to use a gun! What do I *do*?

My questions are answered as the countdown ends. Once my watch strikes zero, my legs move, jerking me forward into a run—I guess that's how I know what to do! I'm kept at a fast pace as I race through the war zone. The robots shoot at me as I run, but thanks to the player, I manage to weave through their bullets and make it through to the fork in the road. From that distance, the player wills me to shoot at the robots. My lack of skill with a gun doesn't seem to be that big of an issue, as the players control over me solves that problem. One by one, I degrade their health with every bullet, and they soon start to disappear in small flashes. It takes quite a bit of time and focus, but eventually, all of the robots with guns have been killed. We did it! We defeated the first set of robots, and I've never even held a gun before! I smile brightly in my head, but the player forces me to continue my run on a path from the fork in the road.

That's where things go sour.

A flaming bomb heads right towards me. Shock and fear overcome me as I struggle to comprehend the situation and come to terms with my helplessness. Unfortunately, the player isn't fast enough, and I experience my first death in the game. Pain sears through my nerves as my entire body burns. I try to scream, but nothing comes out. I should be dead by now—why am I not dead? Everything goes black.

I open my eyes to find myself falling through a dark, narrow space again. I'm back in the tube. The familiar slide-like sensation washes through me, erasing any trace of pain. I am exhausted, confused, and completely ready to head back to my sector for the day, but I'm not the one with the choice.

I land back on the pathway. I groan inwardly— not again! I count on taking the introduction to catch my breath, but the player skips through it, so I get maybe a second or two. This time, I anticipate the sensation that urges my legs to run. I dodge the bullets again and defeat most of the first set of bots, but then a sparkly floating object I hadn't even noticed catches the player's eye. I am willed by the player to swipe my hand through it and a burst of energy surges through me—I got a power-up! With one perfect shot each, I kill the rest of the robots in seconds. TBut before long, the energy disappears and my aim begins to falter. The power-up has worn off.

There are several types of power-ups hidden throughout the battlefield. This one must have been the "weapon skill" bonus, but there are also power-ups for invincibility, super-speed, invisibility, and more. They are pretty difficult to find—especially in the midst of the chaos that is a run—but I guess I got lucky.

I suddenly find myself taking a sharp right turn. That's not right; doesn't the player know that we're supposed to continue along the path? I'm heading straight for the edge of the bridge. I try to will myself to turn around, but the player is in control.

And so I run right over the edge of the bridge, even as my entire body screams for me not to.

We were doing so well on this run, too!

I can land on my feet, I try to convince myself. I feel myself frantically flailing my arms and legs as I plummet to the ground. It's just like the seemingly endless fall when I first arrived in the game—except the view makes it a million times more terrifying. After another explosion of pain, I am met with darkness once again.

As expected, I'm back in the tube. Relief spreads through me as my pain disappears, but I'm also dismayed. I have to do this all over again, and who knows how many times after that. The tube ends and I find myself back in the starting place. Again.

I run and dodge and die and repeat. The runs begin to blur together, and soon I can't even remember how many I've done. All I do know is that each run I get to experience a different way to die. The pain of each death feels worse than the last. Or maybe it's just that the emotional baggage grows heavier with each run. Knowing what it feels like to die in every way possible isn't going to be great for my sanity.

We—the player and I—make it past so much: explosions of hidden bombs, missiles dropped from the air, even shape-shifting robots disguised as foliage. But every time I die, I respawn in that stupid tube.

One particular run scares the crap out of me. Everything starts the same—gun bots, firebombs, missiles—except this time, I get further than I ever have before. Slowly but surely, one by one, I defeat each set of robots. I arrive at the fortress and come face-to-face with the most terrifying creature I have ever seen.

It is made from pieces of scrap metal and so crudely constructed that I can only just make out a rough head, torso, and limbs. Its eyes blast red lasers that seem as if they will slice my skin if the creature so much as looks at me. Its teeth are made of razor-sharp daggers, and its "arms" are outfitted with more rifles than I can count. I die before I can even take a step towards it. The worst part? From my experience playing the game, I know that that isn't even the boss. It's simply one of the guards to the robots' military fortress, which is where you face the *real* boss. That boss…it is way worse than anything you can think of, even when you're just seeing it through a computer screen.

Despite my drained and horror-struck state, I brace myself to respawn in the tube. Instead, I find myself back in the glass enclosure where I started. I stumble out of the enclosure with relief. Even though I know I shouldn't, I ignore the arrows pointing towards my wooden cubicle and collapse on the sofa.

I sigh as my entire body relaxes and sinks into the lush velvet fabric of the couch. All of my pain melts away, and I only focus on the luxurious feeling of the sofa. I've never felt something so nice...

"You have to go back to your cubicle, sweetie! The player isn't done yet, and it's still your shift!" A woman's alarmed voice jerks me from my paradise. I scurry back to the wooden cubicle, ashamed. Once I am inside, I apologize to the lady. I can't believe I did that; I swear I read the rule book!

During most of my feeble apology, I look at the ground to hide my embarrassment. But as I near the end of it, I gain enough courage to look up at her through the glass window. Only then do I notice her eyes. The left one is perfectly normal, but the right one is bright teal. Like, superhuman, robot, alien-from-another-galaxy teal. I can't stop looking at it—it's like the way the game used to mesmerize me. I finally break my gaze and bow my head to avoid making eye contact again. The lady just sighs sadly, like she's used to that by now.

I feel bad, but I'm also sort of scared of her. Instead of questioning my manners, I turn to the person in the cubicle on my other side.

"It's Ada, right? You're the one who carried me when I first landed here! Thanks for that," I say, trying to be friendly to make up for our rough beginning yesterday.

"Yeah, no biggie," Ada replies distantly. She seems...well, sad. Just like everyone else here. It's like all the hope has vanished from their lives. Hope that should have been there. Hope that I want to bring back.

"So, um, who is that over there, and why is her eye so *blue*?" I ask, trying to seem casual, but my curiosity and unease are apparent. Ada snaps out of her daze and reads me like a book. She glances at the woman with kind, pitying eyes.

"That's Luna. Trust me, Luna always has your back. When the GameMaster first started to put real people inside, there were twelve people trapped here. We call them the OGs. And Luna was one of them. She is the last original player of the game still here, still *trapped*."

"What happened to the other OGs?"

"They escaped. Luna stayed behind to pull the trigger that released them." I let out a gasp. So escaping *is* possible! Again, Ada seems to have read my mind. She simply shakes her head and explains how that was the first and only break-out. Now, more advanced programming prevents us from even getting close. It's really high-tech stuff—way too technical for people without any coding experience whatsoever to understand.

Despite her discouraging tone, I refuse to let myself believe her. There has to be some way to get out of here; they just haven't figured it out yet.

"Well, what about her eye?" I repeat, still unsettled by her gaze.

"I'm not exactly sure what's up with her eye, but I do know that it's part of her origin story. I haven't gotten to hear it yet, but I know some people have. I do know that over time the color has gotten more intense, though. Why?" Ada eyes my confused expression.

"Think of being in here for almost thirty years. This game does things to you, Ivy." I nod slowly.

"But what about everyone else? You said the game does things to you—not just Luna," I ask, still attempting to wrap my head around this whole situation.

"I guess so. Not only in physical ways, though. I'm talking psychological damage. I mean, for starters, Crosby used to be a pretty nice guy, at least according to Luna, but after a few years in the game he turned…cold. We see his true colors every now and then, but it's pretty rare. Some of the others use humor as a coping mechanism, but all of us are in the same boat. It's our attitude—our outlook on life. It's always negative. We have nothing to live for, Ivy. I know that sounds harsh, but it's true. There's no hope for us, nothing to look forward to. Just more runs," she finishes softly. I frown, wishing I could pull her into an embrace. Stupid glass wall.

There's no way I can let myself become that hopeless! I have to be strong. For them. In an attempt to distract Ada from her sad state, I find myself asking her all of the questions that I have about the game. Crosby hates having to answer them, it helps take Ada's mind off of things, and I'm actually starting to understand what life in the game is like—if you ask me, wins all around.

"What about that gun? When I went on my runs, I had a gun that I could shoot the robots with, but when I came out of the game, it disappeared," I tell her.

"I almost forgot about that! That's what you call a default weapon. Obviously, you need a weapon in the game, but the programmers haven't had a chance to give you one of your own. For the next few days, you'll have to use that until The GameMaster sends you your actual weapon through the drop tube." I didn't know

I'd be getting a real weapon of my own! That's actually kind of cool.

We wait for a couple more hours in our cubes. I chat with Ada to distract myself from the plodding clock. Ada is so sweet, but her feisty temper never fails to make me smile. She is just the type of person I need here: strong-willed, funny, and brutally honest.

Talking with her, it feels like…well, it feels like I've known her all my life. Ada is so much different than Jane, but the way we clicked immediately is the same. It feels like Jane is still smiling and laughing with me. Like she is still my friend. Like she still cares about me the way she used to.

"Oh, come on! It's not that far to jump!" I exclaimed confidently. The warm air whipped our hair into tangled messes as we continued our climb up the rocky mini-cliff of the park.

"You're insane, Ivy!" Jane yelled as she placed her hand on another ledge. I pulled myself over the edge and stood up carefully on the small area. Reaching out my hand, I helped Jane up onto the rock. Our sixth-grade selves surveyed the park with pride. I high-fived Jane and she laughed.

"A little more practice and we'll be climbing Everest!" she joked.

"Ha-ha. Now you've had enough time to think about it. Are you going to jump with me?" Jane aggressively shook her head.

"Ivy, you're going to get hurt! This is elementary -schooler stuff."

"No, it's fine! Tia did it and she didn't get hurt," I responded, attempting to convince her to join me. Jumping the cliff at the park was the most daredevil thing you could do! This was going to make us the coolest kids at school! Even if Jane didn't want to jump with me, I was going to do it.

"Ivy, no. Besides, it's not like you're actually going to—wait!"

With a burst of adrenaline, I leaped from the edge of the small cliff and flew through the air. For a moment, I felt pure energized bliss.

Then I neared the ground. And I realized just how little I'd thought this through.

Jane's screams meshed with mine as I flailed my arms in terror. I collided with a smash. The small crack that sounded—followed by a fiery pain in my right leg—alerted me that something was terribly wrong. Even from below the small ledge, I could hear Jane's unmistakable yelp of horror.

Faster than I'd ever seen her, she jumped from rock to rock and sprinted to my aid.

"Oh my gosh. Ivy, are you okay? Ivy!?" Her eyebrows knitted in fear. I opened my mouth to respond, but what came out was a pained groan. Her eyes widened. I followed her gaze to find a small piece of bone sticking out of the side of my limp leg. Jane's scream could probably have been heard from across the country.

"Ouch. That looks painful," I whispered, trying to block out the pain with sarcasm. Then I blacked out.

"Hey, how are you doing?" I heard Jane's faint but familiar voice as my eyelids fluttered open. The pain in my leg was mostly numbed, but I could still feel the impact of the crash rattling my bones.

"Where am I?" I squeaked.

"I called an ambulance. You passed out," Jane said quietly.

Obviously. Where else would I be? How could I have been so stupid—jumping off of a cliff for fun? My mom was going to be so mad at me!

Jane noticed my anger at myself and took it into her own hands to distract me.

"Guess what? Brian and Amy posted for you to get well soon on their Snapchat stories! Everyone is going to worship you at school! You're going to be the girl who had enough guts to jump off of a freaking cliff!" she exclaimed. I remained unmoved.

That didn't make me not an idiot. Jane frowned at my still-unhappy attitude.

"Oh, come on! The popular girls and the jocks are going to be so impressed. You'll be a celebrity." I cracked a small grin. That sounded pretty cool. "Also, you know who is going to be so into you after this," Jane teased, referring to Nolan Bushman, my crush at school. She knew how embarrassed I got when she mentioned him! I blushed and swatted at her arm with the little energy I had. Even on the way to the hospital she could figure out a way to get my mind off of things and make me smile.

Jane was with me non-stop for the next three days. Holding my hand during the surgery, spilling the latest school drama whenever she could, making me laugh during recovery, and sharing stories on the ride home.

It made me understand how much she really cared for me. And how much she could make me smile.

I shake my head vigorously in a feeble attempt to break free from my flashback. Jane is gone. Maybe I could have made up with her if I was still in the real world.

But I'm not in the real world. And I won't make up with her, because I am stuck here.

And according to Ada, there is no way to escape.

CHAPTER 5

During my hours-long chat with Ada, a muscular man takes what seemed like a million runs. Every few times, he switches off with the man who encouraged me on my first run. I am getting seriously bored in here. And I'm going to be sitting here every day of my life.

At least Ada has something interesting to talk about: she has a crush on the buff dude taking all the runs. I may never go back to high school, but at least I'll have *some* gossip to keep me busy. To be honest, I'm not really surprised. They would look like a couple straight out of a magazine.

It's only my first shift, but it feels like I've been in this cubicle for decades. And I still have two hours left. My stomach rumbles loudly. This is the longest I've ever gone without food. I spend the next few hours dreaming about my next meal and attempting to formulate an escape plan. I don't get far on the escape part.

A little later, there's a ding and a small light switches from green to blue. Everyone's watches go off. The glass dividers slide up, and I practically leap out in joy. The next group enters glumly. While dancing my way out of the cubicle, I accidentally bump into the same beautiful blonde woman I saw earlier. She glares at me. Then I realize who I've just bumped into. Starstruck, I stammer an apology. After I finally spit one out, her hard gaze softens into an amused smile.

"Jaclyn Casper," she says, and elegantly extends her hand. I shake it in shock and continue to stutter as I introduce myself. After our handshake, she twirls around and struts to the cubicle right as the glass door slides down and her shift begins. I turn my back, and my expression changes as quick as a whip. In an instant I go from outwardly calm to completely ecstatic. I speed-walk to my room and plop onto my bed with a muffled squeal. I can't believe I didn't recognize her at first!

Jaclyn Casper just *shook my hand*!

Jaclyn Casper was my favorite actress for years. She starred in every one of my favorite movies. I knew everything about her. The names of her pets, her favorite colors, her best role—everything!

At the height of her amazing career, she suddenly quit. It shocked everyone. She didn't officially announce she was quitting, though; she just disappeared from the public and the media made assumptions. Little ten-year-old me was heartbroken. I remember wailing to my mom that it wasn't fair that Jaclyn quit.

Of course—she didn't quit, she got trapped in here. But how did a famous model and actress manage to get so addicted to a video game? More than that, how did I not recognize her right away? I guess while I was so overwhelmed and addicted to the game, I barely even registered that Jaclyn had been a player too.

After trying to solve this mystery for a few minutes, I decide to chill out. I could try to work on our escape, but I need to be fully alert for that. My legs are aching and my stomach rumbles louder than ever, so I'm not in a prime position to be focusing on anything important. When am I going to get to *eat*? And how? I should have asked Ada during our shift. I don't want to bother her now, though, so I guess I'll wait until everyone else is ready to eat. I consider reading more of the rule manual, but my eyes begin drooping before I've even opened the book. Instead, I slide under the covers and drift off.

I wake up from my nap to exclamations of relief coming from the common area. I jump out of bed and rush to join the others. I arrive just as a large parcel comes crashing out of the tube affixed to the ceiling and onto the black table.

The man who took all the runs earlier eagerly rips open the package. Out fall five pre-packaged containers of food, each containing a turkey leg and mashed potatoes. Thank goodness—I was about ready to pass out if I didn't eat something soon. I lick my lips hungrily and pick up a container. Somehow it's steaming hot. I sit down next to Ada in the common area as everyone begins digging in. I listen closely to their chatter.

I sink my teeth into my first bite with a grateful sigh. Even though I expect it to taste like cafeteria food, I've gone without food for almost fifteen hours, and my stomach will take anything it can get. But the turkey is actually very juicy and flavorful, and the mashed potatoes have the same buttery smooth texture as the ones my mom makes for Thanksgiving dinner.

But I'll never see her again. Or any of my family members.

Maybe I should have cherished those moments more.

I snap out of my thoughts. I need to focus on getting to know these people better. Even though I know I will figure out an escape soon, I should interact with them at least a little bit. This is my chance at a fresh start!

According to Ada, the more runs you do, the hungrier you get, but you still get the same servings as usual. She says that I'll get used to it eventually. I'm not so sure; I only did a couple of runs today, but I'm ravenous and worn out.

"Hey, Rory and I haven't met the new girl yet! Well, not officially. I'm Sawyer and this is Rory," a posh-looking young man says brightly. Sawyer was the one encouraging me on my first run earlier, and Rory is Ada's crush! I introduce myself and start getting to know them.

Rory, who used to be a high-school football player, is quite boisterous. He tries to present a "tough guy" persona, but he definitely has a soft side. Ada is practically swooning over him the entire time, but I pretend not to notice for her sake.

Sawyer was some sort of world-famous fashion designer prior to getting trapped in the game. I was just thinking about how much I used to love fashion; maybe I have more in common with these people than I think! Obviously, Sawyer is handsome and stylish, but I think his personality is the best part about him—he's hilarious and full of sarcasm.

They both seem like nice people. I must be so boring to them. Here are two people with super-interesting backstories, and then there's me, a teenager who got dumped by her best friend. Even *I* wouldn't want to listen to my backstory.

After dinner, I talk with Rory for a little while. We discuss my first day in the game for a few minutes, but I'm impatient with this small talk. I jump right to my burning question.

"So...Ada?" His face turns tomato red, and he begins stuttering some gibberish I can't understand. I laugh. My intuition is correct: they are made for each other.

I head to my room and immediately crash into my bed. I'm sore from all the running—and dying—but I assume I'll have to get used to that. I fall asleep as soon as my head touches my pillow.

I wake up to my wristwatch blaring a monotone alarm. For a few seconds, my memory is fuzzy and I don't know where I am, but then all of yesterday's events come flooding back into my mind. I groan, but I manage to drag myself out of bed. Here we go again.

12 HOURS LATER

"The first run is the hardest"—I don't know what Sawyer was talking about! Today was just as miserable as yesterday, only this time I had to do it all while super-sore.

I woke up this morning and left my room half-asleep to look for my brother. It's only been a day without my family and I am already feeling homesick. A day! How am I going to survive this? These people are nice and all, but they're little more than strangers. And I don't exactly have a great track record with friends.

All I want is to go home! I wish I'd never bought that stupid pack.

1 WEEK LATER

It's been a full week and I've made no progress on an escape plan. Not even one good idea. I've been spending all of my free time trying to formulate something, but every single idea that I suggest to Ada is immediately shut down. How am I supposed to get us out of here?

I'm beginning to feel as hopeless as the rest of the crew.

1 MONTH LATER

I am trapped in an endless maze with a million twists and turns. I don't know how anyone can handle this. The only thing keeping me sane is my friends. Without Sawyer's lively personality and Ada's charm, I couldn't have survived the first month. At first I really didn't think that I was cut out to make new friends, but I was pleasantly surprised by everyone's open natures. Any time I'm feeling down, everyone is there to cheer me up. It's nice to have people to depend on after so many months of loneliness, but I wish it could have been in a different situation.

As for living inside the game, things aren't going too well for me. I'm getting cabin fever with no "great outdoors" to cheer me up, no wide open spaces, not even something as simple as a movie theater to get my mind off of things. The only time I get to escape our living space is during the runs, and those aren't what I'd call enjoyable. Don't even get me started on those horrible wooden boxes that we're forced into twelve hours a day. The boredom eats away at me until I want to scream. The others reassure me that it was like that for them at the beginning too, but I can't help but feel like the odd one out.

I still have the tiniest spark of hope that we can escape, but mostly I spend my time waiting until the next break between shifts. That's all there really is to look forward to.

CHAPTER 6

1 YEAR LATER

I awaken to the familiar blare of my watch's alarm. I hop out of bed and head to the "kitchen" (the black table under the food chute) to pick up today's breakfast.

Not much has changed in the last year; the only big difference is that Rory and Ada are together. I'm pretty sure everyone saw it coming except them. Their cuteness is enough to make me jealous. Other than that, things are more or less the same. I've pretty much gotten used to the way things are around here.

Rory and I share some small talk while we chow down on our bacon and eggs. There's about an hour and a half left before my shift, so I decide to practice in the combat room once I'm done to pass the time.

The combat room is where you train with the weapon that you're assigned when you first get here. After I arrived, I was told that my weapon would be delivered via the drop station like I was—I wouldn't be allowed to choose what I used. It would be chosen for me. Just like everything else in the game. Sure enough, a set of throwing knives fell through the drop chute a few days after my arrival. Ada teaches combat classes for the newbies; she trained me to handle my knives with skill and precision. I was terrified of them at first, but over the time I've trained with them they've become my favorite asset.

I throw away the remains of my breakfast and head towards the combat room. It's a small, dimly lit area with four battered targets and a dummy hanging limply in the corner. I walk into the room and pause to examine myself in the mirror. Before entering the game, I was a scrawny teen—no muscles whatsoever. Thanks to all the physical activity, I'm now almost as muscular and strong as the rest of them. I'm not *quite* there yet. My hair is unbrushed and tangled, but it's gathered into a small bun on the top of my head to keep it out of my face and hide the mess it really is. My face looks worn out; I look different without the fire I once had in my eyes. For the first couple of weeks—months, even—I refused to give into the idea that there is no way out of here. It took a long time for me to give up, but once that fire went out, it was gone for good. My focus shifts as Rory enters the room, rifle in hand.

"You know you can't shoot in here, right?" I remind him, amused. He rolls his eyes at me and holds a finger up to his mouth as if to say "shhh!" I sigh, knowing all too well what's going to happen next. He backs up to one end of the room and aims his gun at the target furthest away from him. I plug my ears. A loud gunshot rings through the air and the bullet pierces the center of the target. He smirks at me.

A second later, several angry yells sound from the hallway, in unison.

"RORY!"

I cross my arms and shoot him the most "I told you so" look I can muster. He rolls his eyes, but instead of mocking me, lunges for my throwing knives.

"Hey!" I yell. Unfortunately, my reflexes aren't fast enough, and Rory snatches the knives right out of my hands. I glare at him. What is wrong with him? I need my knives! He tosses me back half the set of knives (I scold him for his recklessness) and twirls one of the other four.

"I challenge you to a knife-off," Rory says.

"That's not even a real thing!" I exclaim, none of my annoyance subsiding. I snatch angrily for the rest of my knives, throwing away any sort of technique I'm supposed to use. He sidesteps my "attack" with ease, and I end up nowhere near him.

"Come on! It's so boring around here. We need more entertainment!" he pleads. I scoff at his weak argument. No way am I doing something that childish. "Why not? Are you…chicken?" he whispers dramatically. I freeze for a few seconds to rethink my decision. Eh. What have I got to lose?

I whip around and fling one of the knives at his arm. It catches his sleeve, pinning it to the wall—just the effect I was looking for.

"You're. On."

Rory wastes no time, hurling a knife at my legs. I jump just in time, the satisfying sound of the knife slicing into the wall fueling my adrenaline. I haven't had a good old-fashioned fight like this since the combat classes right after I arrived!

I pluck the knife from the wall and throw two at once, aiming for both shoulders. Rory ducks, and the knives nearly graze his ears.

The next thing I know, one heads straight for my torso. I dive for the floor, adding a forward roll for some spice. I hear a whistle from behind us that is definitely Sawyer. I didn't realize we had an audience! Taking advantage of my low stance, I hurl one knife after another at Rory's shins. He sidesteps like a ballerina, tiptoeing delicately as the knives stab into the wall.

After a few more minutes, almost everyone is standing around us, cheering one of us and booing the other. Luna even makes a sign to cheer for me—a sign! For a stupid game that has lasted ten minutes!

Despite the enthusiastic encouragement, we are both beginning to get tired. Our throws are sloppy and misplaced, and our dodges are slow. But neither of us will let the other win. The cheers soon turn into heckles and whiny complaints. Ada, obviously, is simultaneously the most amused and the most annoyed, playfully whining and complaining the loudest out of everyone.

I admit, our throws are starting to get extremely lazy. Just a few seconds ago, Rory's knife hit about five feet from where I was standing. It's clear to everyone else that our match is well past over, but neither Rory nor I will accept defeat.

There is no way I wasted my whole morning to let him beat me! My next lunge is so far from Rory that both of us have to resist the urge to laugh. This is getting comical.

Immediately following my extremely misdirected lunge, I hear Ada get up and mutter something. Her footsteps grow louder and louder, but Rory and I are too busy fighting to care. She's probably just trying to distract us. The next thing I know, I'm lying on the ground next to Rory. Both of us are pinned to the floor by swords. Ada's swords.

"There! Now I win," she says smugly. Rory turns his head to me and mouths, "She's really good!" I laugh and Ada rolls her eyes. She plucks the swords from where they have pinned our sleeves to the mat and helps us up.

"If you two stopped refusing to let one another win like bickering siblings, maybe I wouldn't have had to do that!" she teases. I open my mouth to argue, but I have to admit that she's sort of right.

Ada has described my friendship with Rory perfectly: we really are just like a pair of annoying siblings.

A flash of a memory takes me back to play-fights with my real brother, Chad, and I sigh sadly.

My heart hurts at the thought of Rory replacing Chad. The game has taken over every aspect of my life and made it into something of its own. I love Rory, but no one could ever take the place of my little Chad. I brush the sentimental thoughts from my mind and chuckle at Ada's remark.

We walk back to our rooms together with the hope of fitting in a quick shower before our shifts.

"See? Wasn't that fun?" Rory says happily. I give him an amused look.

"You're an idiot," I reply, avoiding the actual question. No way am I going to admit that I actually enjoyed it a little.

"That reminded me of a competition I had when I was younger," Rory comments, deep in thought. We are already at our rooms, but I can tell this is going to be a story I want to hear.

"Oh? Do tell," I encourage, taking a seat on the floor in my room. After a second of thinking, he joins me.

"Eh, it's kind of stupid, but whatever." I shrug reassuringly. Something being stupid has never stopped him before! "So I was a pretty competitive kid, and my friends were too. One day, one of my buddies decided to make up a challenge. Whoever played the most hours of this one video game by the end of the month won $100." Oh… this isn't just any random story—it's Rory's game origin story.

"I thought for sure I could win. I liked video games, and I *loved* winning! In the middle of this competition, I was facing quite a few family problems. My parents were arguing every night and getting divorced soon, so naturally, I wasn't doing the greatest. I immediately fell in love with *Escape the War*; it just really spoke to me! As the month went on, my friends got more and more tired of playing the game, but I was set on winning no matter what. My parents' relationship was getting worse and worse; I wanted to talk to them as little as possible. This competition was my excuse." Wow. I can't believe this.

"My friends were getting really worried about me. I'd skip school to play the game, sleep as little as possible, and not hang out with anyone. I couldn't stand seeing my mom and dad hating each other, and when I fell behind on school-work…well, everything went downhill from there. The custody battle between my parents was the breaking point for me, I think. Everything was happening so quickly that it was too overwhelming to keep up with—the only thing that I could depend on was *Escape the War*. By the time I got transferred into the game, the competition was long gone—and so was my parents' marriage."

"Dang. That's rough," I say quietly. He waves his arm dismissively like it's no big deal, but I know otherwise. I pat him lightly on the shoulder to show I understand, then get up to go take a shower. Rory has never really been the emotional type, and I've got the feeling that he doesn't want to dwell on his game origin story. I respect that.

All of a sudden, we hear two synchronized beeps from our watches. Rory groans. We forgot about our shift!

Rory and I have made the mistake of fighting and talking right before our shift, tiring ourselves out before the day even begins. We jog towards my sector and make it there just as the second shifters are exiting. I wave to Jaclyn, who smiles in return. She is panting hard and dripping sweat. It must have been a hard day for her.

I sigh as I walk into my "chamber of doom." My hands graze the sliding glass door as I position myself inside the small area. Crosby sighs as his watch begins to emit the loud beep that we all know by heart.

This is my least favorite part of the day and the reason I hate this place so much: you're either overexerting yourself taking run after run in a literal *war zone*, or you're sitting in a cage for twelve hours. Throughout my year in this…prison, I've managed to memorize the ABCs backwards, plan out every aspect of my dream life up to ninety-four years old (and by every aspect, I mean *every aspect*), and learn every single thing about everyone in my shift. We even played a game once to test who knew the most about Luna (spoiler alert: Crosby won).

We've figured out basically everything that's physically possible to distract us when we're in our cubes, but mostly I sit there thinking. Thinking about my family. Thinking about my friends. Reviewing all of my memories with them in my head, over and over again, so that I don't lose those cherished moments.

My biggest fear is that I will eventually forget—forget everything and everyone that was once important to me—and all I will know is the game. I refuse to let that happen. What scares me is that I can already see it taking over. Like just a few minutes ago—the comparison between Rory and Chad! The worst thing I can imagine is that kind of memory override happening with *every part of my past life*.

Although there have been a few blips, I remember almost everything about who I used to be. It's a small victory over the game, considering it has literally taken over my life, but at this point, I'll take any little boost of happiness that I can get.

When I first arrived here, I thought that the player controlling me was the weirdest and scariest thing ever. I would spend my runs trying to break free of the player's hold with all the strength I had. But now, I'm usually just resigned during my runs. Why waste my energy? Not being in control of myself has become the norm. It's not even odd anymore.

In this shift, I take about ten runs at the beginning and five at the end. That's a pretty typical day for me as "Ivy." We don't get many "full breaks," when none of the characters take runs because no players are on the game. Players of *Escape the War* are usually pretty heavily addicted. They play as much as they can. Hence, hardly any full breaks. Luckily, today we have a full break for a few hours. We have a great time enjoying each other's company; it really isn't as bad as usual.

The shift seems to end a little more quickly than usual, and the loud *boom* of the sliding door jerks us from our conversation. Jaclyn and I exchange tired smiles as we switch, and I head straight for the kitchen with everyone else. Rory tosses the parcels out of the food chute quickly, and each of us grabs a pack.

I take my spot by Ada on the couch and devour my food. Another reason I despise living in the game: when you're on shift, you can't eat anything for twelve hours. *Twelve hours* with no food! Despite the hundreds of days I've spent here, I still have trouble with that rule. I get hungry really fast, and that length of time between meals isn't the easiest thing to adjust to. That's why our first meal after our shift is quick and quiet. It sometimes lasts only five minutes.

I quickly finish my tofu sandwich and chomp down the fries in just a few bites. Everyone finishes around the same time, and we go our separate ways. There are only three or four hours until the "recommended bedtime," and we all have little things we like to do in our free time. Of course, there are many limitations on our leisure activities—simply because of the constraints of living in the game—but we get creative.

My first day here, I couldn't believe that everyone *made* their own items for activities. But with time and experience, I too have become decently skilled at improvising stuff out of leftover materials.

The activities that we enjoy alone are peculiar. Maybe not *peculiar*, but unexpected for our personalities—for example, Rory works out a lot, but he also likes to write. He's written stories and articles; he's even working on a book. Other people like memorizing trivia or inventing things. Napping is a popular activity for everyone!

I love playing and making up games. That's where my "inventing" skills come out. I've made a deck of cards, replicated a few board games, and even made up my own: a combination of *Connect 4* and *Scrabble*. I still need to figure out a name for it...I'm thinking of "Word Scramble" but it feels a little boring. At least I've got plenty of time to figure it out. My opponents vary, but no matter who I play with, it's fun to try "old-timey" games like poker or spoons, too. And I never lose.

On rare occasions we have "group activities" during free time. These dreaded hour-long ordeals are usually a class of some sort taught by one of us who did said activity before getting trapped—such as Luna teaching dance (I am absolutely dreadful), Sawyer teaching modeling, and Ada teaching soccer. We all pretend to hate group activities, but I actually think they are a lot of fun.

"BS!" Sawyer exclaims, my guilty face giving me away.

"Dang it," I mumble as I pick up the large pile of cards that has built up over the past few minutes. I thought I had him on that one, too! Sawyer moves his hand to place down his next makeshift card, but I quickly stop him. "Uh, no you don't! If you're going to make me pick up all these cards, then you have to give me time to organize them!" I insist, smirking. Sawyer raises his eyebrows at me and leans back to wait.

As I begin placing the cards in order, a few thoughts cross my mind. I know that Sawyer was a world-famous fashion designer; I wonder, did he ever meet Jacyln before the game? I wouldn't be surprised. Famous actress, famous fashion designer…they have to have run into each other before.

It's a long shot, but what do I have to lose?

"Hey, Sawyer! Did you and Jaclyn ever, you know, interact before the game?" Sawyer laughs slightly.

"'Interact'? Really?" he teases. I punch his arm playfully. "Okay, okay, jeez! Yeah, I styled her for a few carpets and runways, and we actually got to be pretty good friends. I learned a lot about her. She started playing *Escape the War* because she hated all the attention. Then the media started overanalyzing our friendship, her addiction to the game got worse, and everything went sour from there. We stopped talking. But when I arrived in the game, I was so happy to see a familiar face! We've rekindled the friendship since then."

"Huh. I guess it must have been strange seeing her in here, right?" I ask, deep in thought about what he just said. Sawyer laughs again.

"You'd be surprised at the amount of 'weird' stuff I've seen. That was nothing!" I stare at him, dumbfounded. How is that *not* weird? If I'd seen an old celebrity friend inside of a video game with me, I'd flip out. Of course, that is an oddly specific situation. Sawyer continues, "When I first arrived here, I actually felt lucky. No fans following me to the restroom—yay!" he mocks in a high-pitched voice, causing me to giggle.

"Ew! They actually did that?" I ask, scrunching up my nose at the thought.

"Don't get me wrong, I loved my fans. But some of them were a little…intense," he explains, an exaggerated grimace spreading across his face. I return it as ideas of what his obsessed fans could have done cross my mind. Suddenly I'm grateful that I was not famous.

"Hey, Ivy? While we're on the subject—"

"The subject of what? Fans following you to the bathroom? You've got more stories about that?" I say, giggling. Sawyer rolls his eyes at me, annoyed.

"No, my past, stupid. What I was *trying* to say was, have you ever heard my game origin story?" I pause for a second to think.

"No, I guess not," I say finally. His eyes widen.

"You got a minute?" he asks with a smile. I nod. I know how difficult sharing these stories is for everyone, but especially Sawyer. It may not have been that hard for Rory, but Sawyer is much more emotional. It would be incredibly rude if I declined his offer now.

"I can't believe I still haven't told you mine." I give him an amused smile. "Well, anyway. It all happened about ten years ago. I was at a great point in my career, and I was making some pretty good cash," he adds with a wink. This time, I roll my eyes. "Then, disaster struck."

Sawyer's face changes. His bright eyes become dimmer, sadder. It's like the *Sawyer* has been knocked right out of him. These origin stories really are painful. I place my hand on his, and he gives me a pained smile before continuing.

"Okay, that was a bit dramatic. But anyway, my mom had been in critical condition for weeks, and she finally passed away. I was only seventeen at the time, so I didn't really know what to do." I clap a hand over my mouth. "I was sort of in shock for a couple of days. To be honest, I didn't have anyone to talk to. Jaclyn and I had stopped talking before this, and my family wasn't the most supportive of my career. It was really hard, but I barely had any time to process the situation. There was a high-profile red carpet event in a week, and I didn't have a dress for my client yet!" he says, theatrically. I crack a small smile.

"It was a good distraction, I guess. But my mind kept wandering back to my mom. Okay—it wasn't my best design. I'll admit it! When I went to the event, the media tore it apart. The fashion journalists found every flaw in the design. My client was furious and fired me right after. I got no bookings for weeks; the fashion media had made me into a joke. I was overwhelmed with emotions: sadness, fury, frustration…I didn't know what to do." Sawyer pauses his story, thinking over the right words.

"It wasn't really the hate from the media. It was the fact that no one cared what I was going through. I wasn't even a legal adult, my mom had died a week ago, and instead of being consoled by anyone, my career had basically been destroyed by heartless critics. Then I found the game in my apartment; I thought my brother had left it behind after his last visit. At first, I played to get my mind off of my real issues, but it became a lot more than that. It was like an escape—"

"An escape from reality," I say quietly. Sawyer nods.

"I didn't have to focus on anything while I was playing. I became reliant on it; I needed to be able to play every second of the day. I assume you know how it escalated, and the rest is history, I guess." I sit there silently for a few seconds. Wow. I had no idea.

"Thanks," I reply, looking at him gratefully. Even though it happened so long ago, I can't imagine the Sawyer I know going through such horrible things.

"No, thank you! It's been years since I had to talk about that. Sometimes it's helpful to remember the hard times because they made me who I am today." Huh. I never thought of it like that. Leave it to Sawyer to take an optimistic outlook on even the darkest of origin stories. "Now, haven't you had enough time to organize your cards?" he teases. I roll my eyes again. Sawyer really is just the person I need to cheer me up.

After I play (and win) a final game of BS with Sawyer, I head to bed. It's a little early, but some extra shut-eye won't hurt.

I jump in the shower for a quick rinse, brush my teeth, and hop into my covers. I turn off my light and plop my head onto my pillow with a sigh.

Today was a long day. I should really get some rest. I toss and turn in my sheets, trying to get comfortable. I close my eyes, expecting to doze off immediately, but I'm wide awake. I try again, readjusting the covers once more—but no, I'm still not even a little sleepy. I groan in frustration. I usually fall asleep as soon as I get to my bed, but tonight I'm just too excited. It's been months and months since something this big has happened here.

Tomorrow, for the first time in 364 days, there is actually something interesting going on. The time has finally arrived. We're getting a new character in the game.

CHAPTER 7

I wake up bright and early, ready to start the day. I grab breakfast (toast and jam) before going around to everyone's rooms to make sure they're awake. It's sort of my thing. We wouldn't want anybody missing their shifts, would we?

On the surface, missing your shift might seem like a great idea: you get an entire day free, get to hang out with the second shifters, and you're not stuck in a box with nothing to do for twelve hours. But, sadly, that's not the case. When I first arrived, Crosby warned me about the dangers of not following the game's rules.

According to him, anyone who has ever tried to skip their shift disappeared mysteriously overnight. I know that means that they died.

I'm too attached to each and every person on my shift to let that happen to any of them. If someone accidentally slept in even once, they would be gone forever. We are way too dependent on each other to deal with something as traumatic as that. Crosby and Luna are the only people who have experienced the disappearance of a shift member—and multiple times, too! I like to take preventative measures, just in case someone sleeps through their alarm.

Plus, today we have to wake up extra early, and the earlier the wake-up time, the more likely it is that someone is still sleeping.

After making sure everyone's awake, I walk back into the living room to make small talk with the others. We chat blandly about the latest update to the game, but it's obvious that we're only talking to distract ourselves from the thing we have been looking forward to for weeks.

The arrival is happening today. Someone is going to fall through that tile in the ceiling just like I did on the same day last year. And their entire world is going to be turned upside down.

A chill goes down my spine as I remember the horror of that day. I can't believe it's only been a year; I feel like I've aged decades being trapped here. One year ago, I was a depressed teenager, and now I feel like an adult. It's unbelievable how much I've changed.

After we eat, everyone disposes of their dishes in the trash chute and expectantly lines up by the delivery zone. Even the people on shift are peeking through their cubicle doors, awaiting his or her arrival.

The next few minutes are silent. Ada anxiously checks her watch every few seconds, and in the corner, Crosby quietly talks Rory through the "game plan." I didn't find out until months after my arrival that Rory was supposed to catch me when I fell so that I wouldn't break all of my bones. The gang was running late that day, so I was caught by the ground—yay for me. We aren't going to make the same mistake this time.

I am practically oozing with curiosity. Is it going to be a boy or a girl? How old will they be? Maybe they will be super shy…or super talkative! Everyone here is so drastically different that nobody knows what to expect when a new player arrives. It's a total toss-up.

The ceiling tile suddenly drops open on a hinge and faint yells echo down the tube. The six of us jump in surprise and scramble to our spots. We hold our breath as the volume of the screams increases. Rory steadies himself under the drop area, his arms wide and ready to catch the falling person. A figure plummets into his arms, making all of us jerk backwards in reflex. Rory expertly catches him or her and carefully lays the person on the common-room sofa. We crowd around the person eagerly as their eyes flutter open.

It's a girl, and she has black hair in a short, uniform cut. Her skin is olive toned, and she has striking hazel eyes. They are mostly brown, but they're dotted with a bluish-grey color. Her eyes seem so familiar to me, but I can't quite place where I've seen them before. It *has* been a year since I've seen anyone from the real world, so can you blame me?

She bolts up from the sofa like she's coming back from the dead. We all jump again, surprised by her speedy recovery from the trauma she just endured. When she notices us, she cringes back in fear, but doesn't react with panic as I did. She's guarded—it's as if she has let a wall slide down. I can see it will take a while to coax her out from behind that wall.

Crosby walks over, calms her down, and proceeds to give her the welcome speech that he has made probably a dozen times over. It is almost identical to the one I heard last year. But this year I am on the other side of the situation.

"Oh…okay," she replies quietly after Crosby is done talking. Wow. She accepted that whole monologue *way* faster than I did. And judging from Ada, Sawyer, Luna, and Rory's faces, they are shocked as well. But we dismiss it easily; she looks like a dreamer who would find stuff like this possible. Maybe even *fun*. After the commotion dies down and Crosby has finished with the tour and introduction video, I go over and introduce myself. Oddly, it doesn't feel like much of an introduction; I really feel like I already know her from somewhere.

There's just something so familiar about her. Is it her face? I doubt it; I've never seen anyone with a nose that perfect. Can it be her hair? Definitely not; that style was not common back in Texas. Maybe her voice? I realize I'm grasping at straws. There is *something* about her, even if I don't quite know what it is yet.

"Hi there, I'm Ivy! Nice to meet you," I say while shaking her hand, making sure to flash a kind smile. I know how hard it is to be the newbie. I want to be her "Ada" and make sure she feels as welcome as I did upon my arrival. (Or, more accurately, as welcome as Ada made me feel once she'd cooled down following the whole napkin-tally fiasco.) She glances up shyly, only meeting my eyes for a second.

"J- Juniper," she says shakily, returning my handshake with something that's closer to a quick swipe. We shuffle around in silence for a few seconds. It's awkward, to say the least. She is way too shy to start a conversation herself, so I give it a go.

"Well, I guess telling you a few things about myself can't hurt. Um…I'm sixteen, I used to live in Texas, and I'm…" I don't know; what am I? "I'm…trapped in a video game?" I end feebly. I wince. Wow, I am not good at this. She stifles a laugh and shoots me a small, amused grin. I return it with my own cheery smile. Now we're getting somewhere!

"But really, what do you want to know about me?" I ask, attempting again to spark conversation. She considers.

"Any…siblings?" she asks. I nod. A sad smile spreads across my face.

"One brother—his name is Chad." And so it goes. We play Q&A until almost an hour has passed and I've spilled just about everything about me: what my life was like growing up, my favorite things when I was younger, dream pets. I'm surprised to find I love it. It refreshes my memories dulled by the game with brighter memories from my childhood.

When my answers finally run dry, I try to convince her to tell me something about herself. After lots of hesitation and more urging from me, she finally complies.

"Um…well…I'm fourteen and a half, I live in San Diego, and I have two little sisters," she says quietly. It's a start! I follow her example and begin prompting her with questions. I ask her everything I can think of, firing questions faster than she can answer them. I think of those little "get to know you" quizzes we did in middle school, and honestly, I feel like a talking version of them. I hope she isn't annoyed. When I finally ask about her hobbies, her response blows my mind.

"What are you good at? You know, talents? Hobbies you like doing in your free time?" I ask.

"I love coding. Last month I was invited to Apple headquarters to fix a glitch in the newest iPhone. I won some worldwide coding competitions…only four years in a row, though. Um…I beat the world record for fastest hack. That was cool. It's just something I do for fun." Whoa! I'm super impressed— we have a real smarty-pants on our hands.

And then it hits me. Stuck in a video game plus really good coder equals…an escape. My jaw drops.

No. Way.

I can't believe our luck. It's as if an angel has fallen from the sky—right out of the drop tube! A programming genius just arrived in the video game that we have been trying to escape for years. Invitations to Apple HQ? Beating world records? It almost reminds me of how Jane used to be…but I don't want to think about Jane now. If Juniper can figure out the game's programming, I'm sure she can find a way to get us out of here—and I don't take possible escapes lightly anymore. I hastily finish our chat and serve her the breakfast that we saved for her.

She eats quietly with Sawyer and me for company. The whole meal is just Sawyer trying to break the ice with bad jokes. It really isn't working. The only person who genuinely laughs is Sawyer. I occasionally force a pity chuckle. His best joke, however, causes Juniper to splutter out a soft giggle. I guess we can consider Sawyer's mission a success.

Once everyone else retires to their rooms for the final hour before our shift, I grab Juniper's hand and lead her to the control room in the corner of the living space, near her new room. The control room is basically a huge digital screen stretched across an entire wall of a small room. All of the game's data and coding information can be accessed with the screen—the real nitty-gritty coding stuff. It's almost like a fuse box for the game. It might seem weird that we all have full access to it, but we are only meant to use it if something glitches and we need a quick fix. When we first arrive, we're required to learn how to fix the small glitches ourselves so that the programmers don't have to. Besides, not a single one of us has even a little computer coding or hacking knowledge, so tampering with the game is out of the question, even if we wanted to. We're talking about the most advanced programming in the world.

I always thought it was kind of stupid that we can walk in there any time we want. I mean, we can just waltz right into the control room and start fiddling with the game itself. But we can't even step foot inside the wardrobe. (I learned that the hard way on my first day.) It made no sense to me. Over time, I got a better idea why. Despite the world-class programmers working on the game, having real people inside a video game causes a million tiny glitches, and apparently it's too time-consuming for the programmers to fix them. Also, players buying outfits is a huge source of income, too big for us to be allowed to choose our own. I wasn't really surprised when I found out; that's all everything in the game comes down to anyway: money and efficiency.

Plus, like I mentioned before, none of us have any idea how to code, so the control room hasn't been useful for much else—but now that Juniper's here, we might be able to use it to escape this wretched place.

Juniper initially seems very confused, but understands my point after my long explanation. She realizes that being trapped here is horrible— and that she is our only chance to escape. With our full access to the control room and her incredible coding skills, there is a huge opportunity for Juniper to hack the system. I don't know exactly how, but if she can mess around with the game's coding, maybe she could create some sort of loophole that would finally get us out of here!

I can already feel her mind whizzing, but for the moment, I make her go take a nap. This day can't have been easy so far, and her first shift is in only an hour or so. I decide to get a little shut-eye too; however, my mind has different plans.

Juniper's arrival has given me a burst of hope. Sure, there might only be a tiny sliver of possibility she can hack us out of the game, but it's something! It's been so long since I believed that there is any chance to escape, and now, I actually have faith that I can get back to my old life. Faith that I can get back to the people that I love and miss most in the world.

Summer was just beginning, and my family and I were having the time of our lives at the amusement park. It was the perfect environment for us to hang out! Sugar, adrenaline, and family time.

"We have to go on that one! Look!" Chad yelled, his face practically covered with blue cotton candy. I rolled my eyes and handed him a napkin before my mom could even tell me to. He hastily wiped his face and then resumed his pleading. I looked up to see two identical, side-by-side roller coasters full of loops and twists.

"Why are there two of them?" my dad asked, confused.

"They're racing! Duh!" Chad said, as if it were totally obvious. Wait! An idea swept through my head. This could be good.

"Me and Chad on the first one versus you two on the second one. What do you say?" I proposed with a smile. Chad fist bumped me and we laughed. My parents exchanged glances.

"Prepare. To. Lose!" my mom said, already hand-in-hand with my dad on the way to the waiting line. Chad and I grinned.

"Wait up!" We exclaimed.

After about twenty minutes of waiting in line, it was our turn to get on. Chad and I raced to get front seats, and my dad managed to drag my mom up to the front of their coaster as well. A couple seconds later, we were buckled and ready to go. I caught my mom's eye across the ride's platform and stuck my tongue out at her. She gave me a fake-offended gasp and placed her fingers as an "L" on her forehead. We burst out laughing.

"Welcome to The Splash Racer. Please fasten your seatbelts and keep all limbs inside at all times. Your water guns are located on the side of your car and are now unlocked. Please refrain from squirting the opposing team until the ride is in motion." I gave Chad a shocked look and he shrugged. Water guns? Of course, he just managed to "forget" that this ride happened to have water guns in addition to all of the craziness already going on? Well, I wasn't complaining—I

was a pretty good shot, after all. Mom and Dad were going down.

I carefully removed my water gun from its compartment and brandished it at my dad. He jokingly put up his hands and we shared a smile.

"Get ready!" I held the pistol in my right hand and tightly gripped the handle of the car with my left. Chad gulped and I nudged him playfully. He always got a little nervous right before the ride started, but I could usually help him shake it off pretty quickly.

"We spray them as much as possible," I whispered to Chad. He grinned, and his nerves visibly melted away.

"3...2...1...GO!" the announcer exclaimed. The coaster lurched forward with a start, speeding toward the top of the hill. I immediately went after my dad with my water gun, attempting to spray him as much as I could before we began our descent. A cold squirt of water hit me square in the face and I gasped. My dad's unmistakeable chuckle sounded across from us, so I returned the favor with a perfectly placed giant squirt to his eyes. I laughed triumphantly, but my victory was short-lived. The cars teetered at the top of the hill, and all of a sudden, we began plummeting downward.

A chorus of screams erupted, and Chad's and mine joined them. Another burst of water —clearly coming from my mom this time—sprayed my hair , so I gathered my bearings enough to soak her clothes on our way down. I swear she blew a raspberry at me.

Immediately at the bottom of the hill, we were thrust into a series of loop-de-loops. I tried to squirt my parents, but just ended up spraying water into the air. On the last loop, I was hit with a sharp spritz of water from the wrong side.

"Chad!" I said sternly, trying not to laugh as we finished the last loop.

"Sor-ry!" he exclaimed, his voice quavering as the coaster bumped along. Out of the corner of my eye, I spotted my parents ganging up on us.

"Chad! Come on!" I squealed, aiming my pistol at the pair of them. As we moved along a series of hills and twists, I managed to get in a lot of good shots—but I was also sprayed countless times. I had no idea my parents were so good at aiming water guns! Although I did expect to completely decimate them, the fact that they put up a fight made it a lot more fun.

By the end of the ride, we were laughing so hard that we could barely see who was going to win! Luckily, Chad was alert.

"*Ivy, we're gonna win this!*" *he yelled. I turned my attention to the track in front of me. Sure enough, our coaster slid over the finish line seconds before our parents' did. Cheers spread across our side of the coaster as we pulled back onto the platform. We happily exited the car and waited for our parents to leave theirs. As soon as they began walking toward us, we began flaunting our win. They claimed the race was rigged, but that didn't stop us from rubbing our victory in their faces as much as we could.*

Despite our sopping-wet outfits, we couldn't stop grinning.

"*What are you smiling at?*" *I asked my dad, eying his mischievous grin. He simply shook his head and nudged my mom. She winked at me and gave him an identical grin. I stood there looking back and forth between them, my curiosity growing by the second. What was going on?*

"*You aren't going to win this time!*" *they yelled simultaneously, racing back toward the waiting line. Chad and I exchanged shocked looks. Without a moment of hesitation, I signaled for him to follow me.*

There was no way we were going to accept defeat!

The simple memory almost brings tears to my eyes. I could get the chance to have that kind of bond again. I could be a part of a family again.

CHAPTER 8

I wake from my nap to Juniper staring at me from above. Startled, I jump up and smack my head right into hers. Juniper winces, then apologizes. Apparently she's a little nervous about her first shift, and she wanted someone to reassure her. I laugh it off and start getting ready myself. I lead her to the common area, where we join Ada for more introductions. A couple minutes later, we hear the ringing of the alarm and line up next to our designated stations. Sawyer shows Juniper to her cubicle—which was programmed to appear the moment she arrived in the game—just as the barriers come down.

Jaclyn trades spots with me, and I shoot her a pitying glance. She can barely walk. It must have been a pretty hard day for her. The light changes colors, marking the beginning of our shift. To my left, I hear a loud beeping. I turn my head to see poor Juniper's terrified face. I try to give her a reassuring look as she teeters nervously to the run tube. She stands there silently as the clock counts down. We all give her quick shouts of encouragement, and then she falls down the seemingly endless black hole. As usual, the black screen flashes to a view of the game, following Juniper's first run.

I feel for her—I remember the terror of my first run and the pain of the first couple of deaths. Being a newbie here is really hard; I hope she adjusts quickly.

She seems to be doing okay, and after a couple more runs, she appears again on the platform. Clearly worn out, she struggles to make her way back into her cubicle before the divider closes up again. We chat quietly about how her first runs went, and it sounds like they weren't terrible. I guess that's one good thing.

Several long hours of talking, explaining, and gossiping later, we leave our stations and once again trade shifts. This is our boring, predictable life. I let Juniper rest for a bit and go to chat with Ada. It has been a little while since I've talked to her, and I haven't gotten the chance to tell her about our possible escape route.

"Ada, I found our escape! We can get out of here!" I whisper. She raises her eyebrows, but leans in further to listen. Ada knows that I'm not the hopeful newbie I used to be, so if I think I have an escape plan, it has to be at least sort of legit.

"Juniper, she's a- a- genius!" I blurt out. Ada looks surprised and a little confused. I try to gather my thoughts before I elaborate. "She's one of the best programmers in the country! It's unbelievable; she's a coding mastermind! If she can hack the system in the control room, we could get out of here. We could go back to living our lives like *normal people.* She's giving us the chance we never thought we'd have!" I need to rein it in—I sound just like I used to when I bragged about my super-genius then–best friend Jane. Not everything is about her!

Unfortunately, Ada's face does not reflect my enthusiasm. In fact, it's the opposite; she's clearly skeptical. I see the doubt running through her mind and try to project how much real hope I have.

"Listen, Ivy, I know you want to get out of here, but if some kid drops out of the sky, acting all innocent while somehow being the next 'Ada Lovelace,' then something is up," Ada says doubtfully. I frown and hold out my hand to stop her.

"What are you trying to say about Juniper?" I ask defensively, narrowing my eyes. I know I just met Juniper, but there's no need for Ada to be so…suspicious.

"Relax! As much as I'd love to believe she's legit, I'm just saying: if something seems too good to be true, then it probably is. Juniper might just be some video game–obsessed kid trying to wow you by exaggerating her 'rad' skills." She puts down her finger quotes. I ponder her words carefully and end up agreeing with some of them. Maybe Juniper did just want to sound cool. Then again, she doesn't seem like the type of person who cares about stuff like that. It might take a little while for me to validate her big claims, but I don't mind waiting—we've made it this long. Well, whatever happens, at least it's something, even if that something is only a little false hope. And if I've learned one lesson during my time in the game, it's that something is better than nothing.

"I know you've been trapped here for what seems like forever, but you have to admit, it's worth a shot," I say, attempting to reason with her. Ada stares at me doubtfully for a few seconds, then lets out a long, tired sigh and nods. I give her a grateful smile and she returns it. Even though it's just her acknowledgment that I *might* be on the right track, it helps my spark of ambition brighten. A longtime character thinks my plan might work! Maybe there really is a chance for everything to come together...

Over the next few weeks, we help Juniper get accustomed to her new (and hopefully temporary) home. I constantly encourage her to work in the control room, and she spends as much time in there as she can. Although Ada's comments shook my faith in her abilities for a little while, Juniper's quick thinking and programming skill have more than gained back my trust. She's easily proven that her smarts are not the slightest bit exaggerated.

After doing some exploratory playing in the control room, Juniper has decided to try to code something new into the program. I have no idea exactly what she's planning to do, but she promises that she will explain it all in detail once she has enough information. I don't mind; we all have faith in her. Often, I sit next to her while she works and pretend to understand the "smart people" language that she rattles off for hours. It really calms me after a long shift, like some sort of therapy.

There are plenty of days when I walk in on her humming or singing; it's nothing unusual. But one day, I bring Juniper a snack while she is working, and the tune I hear coming from the control room is oddly familiar.

It's about an hour after the end of our shift, and snacks are being distributed. We call for Juniper, but she yells back that she's in the middle of something. I grab her an apple and make my way to the control room. I'm about to open the door when I hear the quiet singing that is Juniper's habit while working. But it's different this time. I press my ear to the door and listen closely, attempting to make out the words.

Up, down, left and right, together we will be all right. That's what she's singing. It's childish, but I recognize it: it's Jane's and my old secret handshake! But how does Juniper know it?

I open the door slowly, and Juniper's singing abruptly stops.

"Hey, where did you hear that tune you are singing?" I ask. Her expression remains focused, unfazed.

"It's a thing my little sisters used to sing. I know, it's stupid. But somehow it makes me feel more at home, you know?" she replies. Her eyes are glued to the screen. Of course. She's probably still struggling to transition into being here in the game without her family; it can take a while for some people. Why do I keep thinking that everything comes back to Jane? Jane and I aren't the only ones to ever rhyme a few words—it's just a coincidence. Right?

I push the thought out of my mind. There are more important developments happening!

Juniper's efforts are beginning to attract the attention of the others. Sawyer and Rory are thrilled with the idea that she could find us a way out, and they often check in to see her progress. Ada doesn't seem to be as skeptical anymore—she's even starting to get excited. Crosby isn't happy about anyone toying with the screen in the control room, but Sawyer managed to talk him into giving Juniper the okay. I can tell that Luna doesn't have much faith in it, but nonetheless, she simply agrees, as usual.

The progress is slow but steady. Juniper comes back from her shift, works in the control room as long as she can stay awake, and then goes to bed. In between, my fellow "crew members" and I provide her with food, water, and some company. It's like each of us has a part-time job.

It only takes her a few weeks to come up with a solid working plan. After about four more weeks, she says that she can start to see her vision of the escape. Just from the snippets of code that she shows us, I can tell that she is making so much progress. Another two more months pass, and Juniper says that she is beginning to put the pieces together. After I have a quick chat with her, Juniper decides that it's time to tell the others the full plan. I agree, although I have no idea what the plan actually is. She's explained it to me multiple times, but I've never really paid too much attention, trusting her to think it through. It's always too complicated for me to understand, and she obviously knows what she's doing. The only thing I know is that it involves coding something brand-new of her own. That night at dinner, Juniper gathers us all to explain the progress on her plan for our escape.

CHAPTER 9

"I don't know about this, Ivy," Crosby whispers to me. I shake my head at his skepticism. I know she can make this work. Juniper quietly sits down in front of the six of us and shuffles a few papers. Notes? Really? I don't get why she's so nervous; I'm positive that her plan will be received well. Despite my optimistic outlook, I know that none of us are focusing on dinner tonight. Juniper timidly glances at each of us, then begins to speak.

"I know it has been a little while since this 'plan' began, and I still haven't explained to anyone what I'm actually doing—well, other than Ivy, but I know she never really listens to me." I blush as everyone chuckles good-naturedly. How did she know? She continues, this time a little less tense. "As you all know, I've been spending the past few months coding a special project of my own in the control room rather than tampering with what is already there. The idea that I'm going for will allow the second shifters to escape with us and distract the programmers so that we will have enough time to escape through the tile in the ceiling— all in just a few months!" A round of impressed murmurs spreads. I grin. Juniper's idea really *does* sound impressive. We all wait eagerly for her to explain the full plan. Does it rely on some sort of glitch in the code? Maybe a timing-related trick? Probably something smarter, knowing Juniper!

"Um, the only problem is…well, in order to achieve all that amazing stuff, I- I…" Juniper mumbles.

"Spit it out!" I encourage Juniper, giving her a big smile. What can be so bad about her plan? It's only going to help us.

"I- I have to release a virus into the game!" she blurts.

My heart stops. The room goes silent.

A *virus*. The most painful and practically unstoppable means of death. The thing that would delete all of the game files—and us! And Juniper has just suggested that we *willingly* release one into the game.

Crosby slams his fist down on the table. The small wooden piece of furniture shakes, threatening to give out. He grasps my wrist and pulls me up, staring me dead in the eye. I am too terrified to return his gaze, so I look down at my beat-up black sneakers instead. I will do anything to avoid looking him in the eyes right now.

He grunts angrily and drags me by my wrist into the nearest room.

Once we're inside, a sudden wave of confidence washes over me. I yank my wrist out of his hand and give him a withering glare. He may be mad, but that doesn't give him the right to treat me like a child! Then the door slams behind him, and with the sound, my burst of confidence vanishes into thin air. I want to curl up into a ball and disappear. He is fuming, his face tomato red.

"What are you *thinking*, Ivy? A *virus*!? I was beginning to trust you and Juniper; I thought she was actually getting somewhere. But thanks to your convincing, I've been allowing this girl to construct a *virus*? One wrong move and we all would all be dead in a heartbeat! There's no way we could survive! How could you let that happen?" he finishes, his voice rising to a yell. But I am mad too, and my burst of courage has returned.

"You know what? Dying would be better than staying in this place. Are you *really* going to tell me that you would rather stay here than die trying to find a better life? Crosby, this is our only chance. We're all going to die here anyway. Maybe the reason no one has escaped since the originals did is because they are too afraid to try! Juniper is just trying to give us our *best chance*." My speech ends on a pleading note.

He studies me for a couple seconds before opening his mouth to retort. He has to understand! Suddenly the door creaks open slightly, partially revealing Rory's face. I can hear a few words directed at him in a furious whisper that's recognizably Ada's. They immediately shut the door, and Crosby and I both roll our eyes. Did they really think we wouldn't notice them?

I raise an eyebrow as I open the door wide and sarcastically welcome them in. Crosby's angry scowl scares them off; they both blush and apologize before scurrying away quickly. I can hear Ada scolding Rory as they go. I sigh and turn to face Crosby again. He also sighs wearily, rubbing his temples. I feel like I've aged fifty years during this argument, but we've been in here for barely a minute.

"I don't understand. Why a *virus*, of all things? Couldn't she use something else? Like a harmless little glitch! Or maybe a tiny worm? Or—I don't know—anything *but* a virus? If she is so smart, she should be able to figure out another way!" he says gruffly. I pause. He does make a good point; that was exactly what I was thinking before. I mean, why would she choose something so destructive? All of a sudden, it hits me.

"You really think that one tiny glitch is going to keep a team of incredibly advanced programmers busy enough to miss us exiting the game?" I snap. "Juniper knew that we needed something super detrimental to make sure we had enough time to escape." Crosby chews his lip uncertainly. I give him an "I told you so" look, to which he responds with a mocking scowl.

"Seriously, Crosby. We've tried everything safe at this point. There is nothing left to try! It's our *only chance*!" Silence fills the room as Crosby ponders the options. It's clear that he is stuck between a rock and a hard place. I get it—Crosby has protected everyone in the game for years, and now he is supposed to let them march to their probable deaths? It makes sense that he is hesitant about the virus. But if he doesn't agree to this, we will be stuck here. Forever.

"Fine. You win. Virus it is," he says, throwing his hands into the air. I stare at him in shock. That is not the answer I expected. I was preparing myself for at least an hour of fighting before he gave in! I snap out of my daze and shake his hand quickly, before he changes his mind.

We exit the room to find the rest of the group staring at Crosby—absolutely terrified, of course. He sits down next to Juniper, who immediately tenses and inches away from him cautiously. Crosby doesn't seem to mind.

"Carry on, Juniper," I say calmly. All the heads turn to Juniper, and her mouth drops open. My guess is that I wasn't the only one who didn't expect this quick change in point of view. Juniper attempts to sneak a glance at Crosby, but he notices and encourages her to continue with the plan.

"Oh, um, okay. I won't get into the logistics, but like I said, I release the virus"—I flinch at the word—"which will begin to delete the game files. That will be hugely detrimental to the game, so it will distract all of the programmers. Which then will give us enough time to release the second shifters and climb through the ceiling tile. I'll code a special lock for the tile so that the virus can't get through in case things get out of control.

The tube should lead us to a series of hallways, with a portal at the end. And then, home," she finishes with a deep breath.

It is silent for a few seconds.

"Well, *that* was a mouthful." The room rings in laughter. Of course Sawyer knows just the right thing to say to lighten the gloomy mood.

"So, what stage are we at now?" asks Ada, bringing the conversation back around to serious matters.

"I figured out how to make the virus-proof lock for the ceiling tile and mapped out the virus's path, but those are the easy parts. Now I'm starting the more difficult stuff: developing the virus itself." She winces as the room tenses up again.

"I may be okay with this virus plan in theory, but you keep your experiments and whatnot far away from the gang, you hear me?" Crosby says sternly, closing in on Juniper. I pull him back— Juniper looks even more scared than she did a few moments ago.

"She knows what she's doing," I reply, staring him down. After a little while, his hard gaze softens, and he lowers his eyes. I smirk on the inside; no one intimidates Crosby, it's always the other way around.

The next few weeks are quite boring. Juniper continues to make steady progress on the escape plan, but that's about it for excitement. It almost feels like we're back in the time when we had nothing to look forward to but the end of a shift. It's not the same, though. We all know what's coming—what we're preparing for. And sure, the days are pretty bland, but the calm is nice. It isn't until a month has passed since Juniper's explanation of her plan that something interesting occurs and changes everything.

CHAPTER 10

"Mornin', Sawyer!" I say cheerfully as I pick up my coffee from beneath the food chute. "Breakfast is great today!" he exclaims, his excitement muffled by his enthusiastic chewing. I laugh and roll my eyes. The only person who pays attention to the incrementally different quality of the food each day is Sawyer. Then again, Sawyer is the only one who does a lot of things.

I wave to Rory and Ada, who are enjoying cups of tea. I sigh softly. It's been months since they became a couple, and they are as sweet as ever to each other. They aren't just partners, they are best friends. They have their fair share of arguments—it would be hard not to argue sometimes, given the stress and the tight quarters—but it always ends with them exactly the same as they were before: happy.

Several minutes pass, and I begin to get nervous. Juniper usually comes out of her bedroom almost an hour earlier than I do. She has never been this late. There's no way she could have slept through her alarm; those things are loud enough to permanently damage your hearing. Once I finish breakfast—which, yes, Sawyer, is actually quite good—I hurry towards her room and politely, but frantically, knock on the door.

The door opens the tiniest crack before she throws it open, pulls me inside, and slams the door closed again in a matter of seconds.

"Whoa, Juniper; what is—" I pause as I take in her stressed state. Her tangled hair is falling out of its unintentionally messy bun, and her brows are furrowed anxiously. Worst of all, her beautiful eyes seem duller, fear and stress snaking through them. The dark, puffy bags underneath support my assumption that she has gotten little sleep, if any.

It's strange; her freak-out begins to jog my memory. Her reaction to extreme stress is identical to…Jane's. Ugh! I thought for sure I'd be done thinking about her by this point, and now I'm comparing her to poor Juniper?

I shake my head to clear my thoughts. I open my mouth, but before I even have a chance to ask, Juniper jumps at an answer.

"No! No, I'm not okay!" she wails. I shush her—we aren't alone, and we can't afford to panic the others when I don't even know what's going on yet. Juniper claps her hands over her mouth before continuing, more softly this time. "It was pretty late last night, and I was working on the virus, right?" I gulp. This explanation is not going in a direction I like. "I left for two minutes to ask Rory if he was done using my wrench—"

"Wait, why was Rory using your wrench? Why do you need a wrench to work on code? And how did you even *get* a wrench?" I interrupt. She shoots me a desperate look. I wince.

"That's beside the point! And when I came back, I realized...well, I realized that I, um, accidentally set off the virus."

I freeze. It's as if my worst nightmare has come to life. I feel myself becoming more and more alarmed, then beginning to go into a state of hysteria. I take a deep, shaky breath and allow Juniper to try to explain herself. Maybe it's not as bad as I think!

"It isn't fully formed yet, so at least it will...kill us faster?" she whimpers. I stare at her, horrified. She quickly tries to take back her original sentence and starts differently this time. "I stayed up all night—and luckily, I was able to postpone the release of the virus for a little while. But it's still coming for us, and if I don't figure this out, it will be here in less than two hours."

Right there, I lose control and go straight into panic mode.

"Juniper, you have to spot the virus! We are all going to *die*!" I want to scream. This is the exact situation that Crosby warned us about. She searches for the right words before abandoning the attempt to speak. All she does is nod. She has to fix this. She *has* to.

The next hour is absolute chaos in my mind. I put on a completely calm mask to avoid suspicion, but Ada is not buying it.

"You good, Ivy? You seem a little…off," she asks warily. My fake smile falters, but I try my hardest to keep up the act.

"Oh, everything is…great! Just…great!" I laugh nervously, and my eye twitches. Ada studies my face for a minute before shrugging and continuing her game of cards with Rory. I let out a huge sigh of relief and bolt to the control room, which is conveniently located right next to Juniper's room. As soon as I arrive, I see that her tension has subsided a bit.

"Any...*good* news?" I ask, hope breaking through my stressed demeanor. Juniper sighs with relief and nods, a smile on her lips.

All I can think is *thank goodness*.

I relax as Juniper tells me she has stopped the virus from deleting the game. I have no idea how she managed that—considering that being "unstoppable" is pretty much the point of a virus— but I'm not complaining! I can hardly believe it: we are safe, and we haven't even lost any progress towards our escape.

After we both catch our breaths (the last hour having been *extremely* intense) I urge Juniper to use the last hour we have free to rest. After the trauma we just endured, I think we can both use some sleep. I flick the light-switch off and slowly close the door behind me. I grin as I spot the shy smile that crosses her face before she shuts her eyes. But right before the door closes fully, a flicker of darkness shoots through the room. I blink and reopen the door. I must be seeing things.

"What? What's wrong?" Juniper asks as she sits up. There it is again! I turn the lights back on, ignoring Juniper's pleading questions.

I gasp as the top corner of her room turns pitch black, begins crumbling away, and disappears in a cloud of ashes, leaving a gaping hole of darkness in its place. And it isn't just the corner—the blackness is spreading through her whole room, devouring it piece by piece.

I let out the loudest, most terrified scream I've ever heard, grab Juniper by the arm, and sprint out the door. I slam it with all my strength, almost tearing it off the wall, and keep running. I hear distant, confused yells coming from the others, but I am in too much shock to answer. All I know is that Juniper is beside me and we are running away from *something*.

"I messed up the code!" Juniper half-gasps, half-wails as we bolt through our living quarters. If she messed it up, that means that thing is…the virus!

Juniper didn't stop it—it's already here.

Seconds later, the group joins us, my petrified yells driving our run to nowhere. Juniper mumbles gibberish as her fingers fly across a small device she grabbed from her room before it was devoured. Crosby, the leader of the pack, takes a sharp turn towards a hallway that I didn't know existed. He yanks open a tiny door and stuffs us all inside the smallest and dingiest closet of the living space. Rory slams the door shut, alarming the rest of us—the door isn't exactly sturdy, and Rory is a pretty strong dude. If he accidentally breaks our only chance for survival...

"W- what...was...that?!" Ada whimpers, burying herself in Rory's protective embrace. I ignore her and instead focus on the intense coding Juniper is doing. I silently pray that she will save us all. Crosby is pale and green; he looks ready to puke.

"How long?" he asks hoarsely, directing the question at no one in particular. The room remains silent; not a single person even tries to reply. The only sound we hear is the frantic tapping of Juniper's fingers on her device.

This is really it. We were stupid enough to let a virus be created inside our living quarters, and now it's going to kill us. I should have listened to Crosby. I should never have let Juniper do this. If she can't fix this, right now, then we are all dead.

I believe in Juniper—I really do—but this might be too much for her. She has seconds to stop a virus programmed to destroy everything in its path; it's an impossible task. But there's still a chance. There is always a chance.

At least that's what I have to tell myself.

I'm about to ask how she is doing when she shoots up, takes a shallow breath, and charges through the closet door.

No.

"Juniper! Are you *crazy*?!" I scream after her. What is she doing? What do *I* do?! We can't just let her die! I shoot the others a frantic glance, but they look as shocked and unsure what to do as I am. There is no time to think through this; I need to get her out of there now.

After a second of weighing my options, I whip open the door and start towards Juniper, my fear powering my speed. I hear Ada screaming my name and Crosby shouting a few colorful words. I race through the living space, my only goal getting to Juniper. Everything is flying by me in a blur. My heart is pumping so fast that I feel like it's about to burst out of my chest. All I can think of is the dark shadow of the virus killing Juniper right in front of me, and that is the only thing that keeps me from running right back into the safety of the closet. I am so focused on saving her life that I don't even notice what is going on around me; I can only think of catching up with her.

Once I near Juniper, I realize what is happening and stop dead in my tracks.

The damage that the virus has created has stopped spreading, and some of it is even starting to repair itself. The old sofa—which has been reduced to a pile of ashes— reappears as its ashes morph back into shape. It solidifies and resumes its former red color; then the familiar velvet texture is restored. The crumpled-up walls straighten out and return to their pristine white state, and the rest of the furniture seems to be following suit. The carpets, tables, furniture...they're all coming back together before my eyes.

A smile spreads across my face, and I shout for the others, who warily come out from hiding. Before I can see their reactions, I'm almost toppled over when Ada attacks me with a hug. She squeezes me tightly and exclaims, "I thought you were going to die!"

I don't admit it to her, but so did I.

I apologetically return her hug and wipe the sweat from my forehead. Once she finally releases me from her embrace, I can see that the others are overjoyed at the rebuilding that is occurring. Within minutes, every bit of damage is fixed. I spot Juniper grinning to herself in the corner and walk over to her with a smile on my own face.

"I can't believe it! You saved us!" I exclaim, pulling her in for an embrace. She smiles coyly and holds up the gadget she has been working on. The screen displays a bolded, bright-green message in all caps: FAILSAFE ACTIVATED. I shake my head in wonder.

Of *course* Juniper is too smart to not have a failsafe in case something went wrong. My grin widens, and so does hers.

The others soon thank Juniper for saving us, although Crosby is still mad about her setting off the virus in the first place.

"Look, she said she was sorry!" I plead, begging Crosby to forgive her. He rolls his eyes, but doesn't say anything else. I sigh, discouraged, and begin to start tidying up the mess that was caused by our sprint to the closet. Before long, a question occurs to me and I face Juniper.

"How did that even work? How did you get rid of the virus?" In the moment, it seemed impossible that she could pull it off.

"Well, you remember I kept typing on my gadget thingy?" she asks, attempting to simplify her terms enough that I can understand.

"Yeah," I reply, a memory flashing through my mind.

"The virus was a few new lines of code telling the game to delete everything. So, in order to stop it, I had to write a couple *other* new lines of code telling the game not to delete everything!" she says. Huh. That does seem pretty easy.

"The failsafe is an algorithm I wrote to undo what the virus had done. I know it sounds simple, but trust me, it's not as easy as it sounds!" Juniper adds, a laugh in her tone. She holds up her device, which has a full page of random letters, numbers, and symbols in a minuscule font, all squashed together. I stare at it blankly. Definitely not simple.

"We are really quite lucky!" Juniper says. She receives an annoyed glare from Crosby, who is seething silently. "No, I didn't mean it like that!" she frantically explains. I tell her to ignore him and she continues. "What I *meant* is that if the virus were fully formed, then all the items affected wouldn't just rebuild like that. They would stay black and all crumpled up," Juniper says, with optimism. I give her a happy smile.

"We wouldn't want that to happen, now would we?" I joke.

Ada butts into our conversation, the nervous look on her face foreshadowing her question.

She glances at both of us warily before taking a shallow breath.

"Wait—if you activated the failsafe, does that mean all our progress is *lost*?" She cringes away, anticipating Juniper's answer. Juniper's smile falters, and she slumps over sadly. Only a small nod—that's all it takes to completely wipe the smile off everyone's face. Three months of exhausting effort, incredible breakthroughs, and long work shifts in the control room, all gone.

The same monotone beep we've heard a million times by now blares loudly from each of our watches. We exchange looks and reluctantly climb into our stations. As she passes, Jaclyn cocks her head curiously at everyone's tired faces, but mostly at my drained appearance. I look worse than she does, and she's the one who just did a full shift of runs.

Of course, with my luck, I run about a hundred times this shift. By day's end, I can barely walk. It feels like every single muscle in my body is sore. I can't even breathe properly towards the end. After what seems like years, I finally find myself back by the run tube's entrance. Seconds later, the light switches colors, and I limp out, wincing with each step. Jaclyn gasps as she sees my feeble exit. She scoops me up and deposits me on the sofa. She gives me a smile, then rushes back to the cubicle, barely making it there before the divider slams down.

I'm seeing stars. My head is pounding, and I can't feel any of my limbs. Even though I'm sitting down, I start swaying. I hear the faint sound of Jaclyn yelling for Ada from her sector.

Everything turns black.

"PSST! IVY!" I AWAKEN TO Ada's calm voice and gentle shaking of my shoulder. Juniper and Sawyer are also crowded around me. I blink a few times, then slowly sit up. Whoa—too fast! I immediately lie back down, and the woozy feeling subsides. I hear a chorus of urgent whispers before one of them leaves my side. Sawyer and Juniper gently lift me into a sitting position. This time I don't feel like I'm going to faint.

Ada returns with a small medical kit in hand. She fumbles with the kit's latches before finally getting it open, then unscrews a small bottle and shakes out two pink pills. Sawyer forces them past my lips and splashes some water into my mouth to help me swallow them. I cough a few times but then gulp them down, eager to feel better.

Almost instantly, my dizziness subsides and I feel much better. The foggy feeling in my mind starts to clear and I sigh in relief. Mysterious pink medicine…I think those were the miracle pills—at least that's what we call them. I have no idea how it's possible, but whether it's a broken limb, a headache, a sore throat, or even (apparently) passing out, the miracle pills will restore you to full health right away.! Luna says the miracle pills were magically dropped into the game when it first started, and never once did they not work. I think that it's so that we don't miss a shift if we're sick or hurt. I've heard so many stories about them, but this was my first time actually using them.

I rest as Juniper rambles on about her day. I'm not really listening to what she's saying; it's nice just to hear the sound of someone talking. After whatever it is that I just went through, it's comforting, like a reminder of home. A lightbulb blinks on in my head—another memory resurfaced. It's exactly like the way my brother used to talk to me every day after school. He used to look forward to that so much. Back when I used to spend time with my family.

Back when my family even knew I was alive.

"Chad! I can't talk; Jane's over!" I tossed my backpack on the kitchen table. Jane smiled and waved happily to Chad. At this point, he thought of her as a second sister. I grinned as Jane and Chad did their own secret handshake. Jane was the best.

I could hear my mom talking with her old friends on her phone. Her excessively loud mom-on-the-phone voice rang loud and clear throughout the house.

I chuckled to myself before looking up to find my dad chopping vegetables and small-talking with Jane.

The smell of grilled chicken filled the room, and my dad gave me an exaggerated wink as he pretended to be a professional chef. He tried to turn the chicken over using a fancy technique, but he ended up dropping it on the floor.

I couldn't help it—I burst out laughing. Jane stifled a chuckle, then cracked a joke that made all of us laugh. My mom peeked out from behind her bedroom door and emitted a disappointed sigh at the mess, but even she couldn't hide her smile.

Chad grabbed my leg and looked up at me with the biggest eyes he could conjure. I groaned and pried his arm off me with annoyance. He was reluctant to let go.

"Dad! Can you distract Chad so he will leave us alone?" I asked, trying to conceal my urge to laugh

as Chad attempted to latch onto one of Jane's limbs. My dad rolled his eyes playfully, wagging a finger at me as he gestured to the mess of chicken on the floor.

I groaned and started to beg my mom. Unfortunately, she anticipated what I was going to say and declined before I even had the chance to finish my sentence.

"Come on, it might be fun!" Jane said, trying to be a nice guest. I grimaced and shook my head violently, but Jane was sure that it would be fine.

"Look at him! How can you resist that adorable face?" she urged, playfully squeezing Chad's cheeks. He stuck his tongue out and Jane and I laughed.

Out of options, I finally gave up.

"Fine. Whatever. Give it a go, bud!" Chad's face lit up and he began rambling about his day. His mouth was flying so fast, I could barely keep up. I simply laughed, trying to put together the few pieces I actually caught. I think it had something to do with the jungle gym—and potatoes? Honestly, I was just trying to look like I understood anything that came out of his mouth. I think Jane was trying her best not to laugh.

"And then, recess was over!" Chad finished, out of breath. I stared at him, my dumbfounded expression worth a thousand words. We shared a smile, and I chuckled at his flushed cheeks.

"Did I miss something?" Jane said, obviously as confused as I was (if not more). Her usual smarty-pants look of understanding everything perfectly was thrown out the window. I giggled. She had dealt with Chad's craziness almost as much as I had; this was nothing new to her. Still, seeing the look on her face every time was enough to lift my mood.

"Um. Sorry?" he apologized, shrugging. Jane and I shared a glance and slowly shook our heads in unison. No one could ever be like good old Chad.

And just like that, the memory of a simple, everyday occurrence from the past—the kind I now savor so much—ends. Juniper tells me that she has to go, and Ada arrives to take her place as my "entertainment" while I am recovering.

"Ivy? Are you okay?" Ada asks me, concerned. I nod and then shake away the remnants of my memory. I do feel much better. I glance at her and grimace slightly at her expression. She looks really irritated right now; maybe I should be the one asking her if she's okay.

"Great. Because I really need to rant." I give her a small smile, gesturing for her to go ahead. Knew it! I still have a slight headache; maybe this will take my mind off of it.

"This is going to sound super stupid compared to what w—er, you—went through but I *need* to get this off my chest," Ada starts. She sits on the couch next to me and puts her feet up on the coffee table with a sigh. Sawyer joins us as well, intrigued by Ada's frustration.

"Good. I need more than one opinion anyway," she says, acknowledging Sawyer. He and I share a curious glance. What could possibly be wrong with Ada?

"It's Rory. He's being—ugh—so unreasonable!" she blurts out. I already know that was not what Sawyer was expecting because it certainly wasn't what I was expecting. They fight and all, but this is the first time Ada has needed to straight-up rant about Rory. She glares at our shocked expressions.

"Oh, don't act so surprised. We are in a relationship; there's bound to be problems here and there. Anyway, he is acting like a jerk right now! He says that I'm not spending enough time with him. *Apparently* I spend more time in the combat room than with him!" Sawyer almost snorts out his water laughing, earning an unamused look from Ada.

"It's not funny! I like working out, yeah, but I still spend time with him. He doesn't need to get all offended. I'm not actually a bad girlfriend, am I?" Ada asks. Now I can see the genuine worry in her eyes, and I know how rare that is for Ada. She never takes anything too seriously, and the fact that she is troubled about this shows that it really does mean a lot to her. Even though I know nothing about fighting with a boyfriend, a best friend needs to be able to help with hard stuff like this. I guess I'm playing relationship counselor now.

"Listen, Ada. Rory loves you—it's so obvious. This is one minor issue. You'll work it out!" Her concerned expression doesn't change, and she chews her lip anxiously.

"But I don't know what to do! And what if it isn't just a minor issue? What if he actually wants to break up with me?" I exchange a worried glance with Sawyer. I think she's blowing this a little out of proportion.

"All you have to do is talk to him about it. Explain the problem to him and then you two can work together to fix it. And trust me, we would all know if Rory was planning to break up with you," I tell her. She brightens a little.

"She's right. Just tell him how you feel! I know that probably sounds very un-Ada-like, but you're human," Sawyer adds. Ada visibly relaxes.

"Thanks, guys. I know it's a super small thing. It's just that everyone puts so much pressure on us to be the 'perfect couple.' Sometimes I feel like we aren't supposed to have any issues," Ada admits reluctantly. I get where she's coming from. Relationships are probably hard enough without being stuck inside a video game together.

With this small confession, Ada snaps back out of her pensive mood and back to her normal self.

"Oh gosh, why did I even say that?" she groans, getting up to leave. Sawyer and I laugh.

"You're welcome!" we say in unison.

By dinnertime, I'm feeling much better, and I join everyone for the meal. Juniper, determined to make up for lost time, takes hers while she works. I check on her before bed, and then fall fast asleep.

Weeks pass. Juniper is more focused than ever on the task of coding our escape—and it's paying off. In less than three weeks, she has made up the amount of progress that had previously taken her more than three *months*.

Although everyone is thrilled about her enthusiasm, it's clearly taking a toll. The only time we see Juniper is either in the control room or during our shift. Her sleep is down to about an hour a day. Her eyes are beginning to lose their sparkle and her body is weakening. She'll be exhausted after two or three runs. If she keeps up this pace, there's no way she can handle the months of work ahead. And a tired Juniper means there is more of a chance of the virus somehow slipping out again. Lord knows we *cannot* deal with another one of those instances. One night, we decide to sit her down for a conversation.

"Juniper, we need to talk. Juniper? Juniper!" I exclaim, giving her a pat on the cheek. Her bloodshot eyes fly open. She scrambles up, trying to regain alertness. I sigh. This might take a while.

"I need you to listen to me," I say, emphasizing my words so that she understands the severity of the situation. The longer we ignore the problem, the more complications we risk in the long run, for all of us. She nods her head vigorously as an attempt to rally her droopy eyelids.

"I know you've been making amazing progress the past few weeks, and that's great! It's just—well, we're worried about you, Juniper," I say seriously. I glance at her to make sure she is listening. Her eyes are dazed. I groan. I wave my hand in front of her face and she snaps out of it.

"Sorry! I spaced out for a second there. Um, what did you say?"

Obviously, it takes me some time to explain to Juniper that she needs to start taking better care of herself without her falling asleep during our conversation. I get that she is only running on a little sleep, but it's really frustrating! After almost a half hour and a dozen tries, I finally get Juniper to understand my point, and she promises to take care of her own health. I'm not too hard on her for not doing it originally, but I assure her that we will all be watching her and making sure that she is doing okay.

From that day, our progress slows, but it is worth it a million times over. Everyone's mood seems brighter, and Juniper is beginning to have fun while working on the control room's screen. About two months after our conversation, Juniper explains that the virus is almost ready to be released. Days have been uneventful the past few weeks, so this sudden development gets everyone hyped up. Things are starting to fit together.

CHAPTER 11

"Okay, is everyone here? Well, except Crosby. He would not like it if he knew we are doing this," Rory says, clearly excited for whatever it is we are about to do. A series of tired grunts indicate the answer to his question. Luna, Sawyer, Ada and I have all taken quite a few runs today, and we are not in the mood for Rory's shenanigans.

"Perfect! Follow me." He leads us through the hallway. I sigh, turning to Ada.

"Why do we have to do this now? Can't we at least wait until morning? And where's Juniper?" I whine. Ada laughs at my childish behavior.

"Juniper needs her rest! And please. You can hang on for a few more hours!" My eyes widen. *Hours*? I can barely keep my eyes open as it is! Ada smirks.

"Kidding!" she snickers. I roll my eyes. Ada gives me a sarcastic apology and tells me it will only take a few minutes. Thank goodness.

"Here we are!" Rory announces proudly. The room is small, with a glass divider separating us from the important part. Behind the glass, racks of fancy outfits, protective armor, and dangerous weapons line the walls. There are accessories, jackets, shoes—anything you can think of!

But we can't access any of it unless a player buys something with their coins. This is the character wardrobe I saw on my first day here.

He made us stay up this late to look at the *closet*? Someone starts to slow clap. We all turn to Sawyer—who else would do that? There's an amused expression on his face.

"Great job, buddy! You found the closet," Sawyer jokes, patting Rory on the back. Everyone but Rory chuckles. Sawyer turns around to leave, but Rory spins him back around and pulls out a toolbox.

"We're breaking in."

Rory has had a lot of dumb ideas, but this one is the dumbest by far. I can't stop myself—I start laughing. I laugh and laugh until I can't even remember how long I've been doing it.

"Nice one! I'm going to bed," I declare between chuckles. Breaking into the wardrobe, huh? What's next, climbing up the food chute?

"Wait!" Ada yells as I turn to go. "He's got a point; we do need protection for the escape," she concedes. My jaw drops. Luna and Sawyer nod reluctantly. Are they serious? A quick survey of the room confirms that everyone is, in fact, serious. Great. I let out a sigh and cross my arms expectantly. There are a few moments of silence as the group tries to figure out whether or not I'm going to leave.

"Go on!" I say, unenthusiastically. I'm not going to be the only one left out of this. Even though I'd much rather be sleeping.

"The door only opens when a player has purchased something, right?" he starts, gesturing towards the large metal door in the center of the glass wall. "And we only get the key through the drop chute when the player selects it, correct?" Rory continues. Luna and I glance at each other.

"Honey, I hate to break it to you, but all of this is stuff that we already know. Why are we really here?" Luna interrupts gently, placing a frail hand on Rory's shoulder. Rory nods and fast-forwards to the point.

"If we can pick the lock, we get access to everything!" he finishes with a big smile. I raise one eyebrow. That sounds way too easy. Rory sees my skeptical look.

"I did my research! I swear!" I shrug my shoulders. I guess it's worth a shot. We are each assigned a job. Luna and I are in charge of making the key out of a bobby pin we found lying around, Sawyer and Ada are tasked with making a list of everything we need from the inventory, and Rory is the one actually picking the lock.

Luna turns out to be great company. We work efficiently together, and she's pretty fun to talk to. I've never really socialized much with Luna one-on-one; it's nice to finally chat with her.

"So, how did you learn how to pick locks?" I eventually ask, continuing to fiddle with the misshapen bobby pin. Luna lets out a slight laugh. Her eyes turn glassy, as if she is searching for a memory.

She tells me a hilarious story about how, as a kid, she would sneak into the candy store late at night and take candy. But she would leave money on the counter because she felt so guilty! I'm not surprised—Luna has the kindest heart of anyone I've ever met. Only she would do such a thing.

"I used to go to the candy store all the time with my best friend. Almost every week. We would beg our parents to get us something, and when they did, we felt like we were on top of the world!" I recall happily. Luna smiles.

"You must miss her very much," she says. I shift awkwardly.

"Oh, um…we aren't really friends anymore. Or we weren't, before I came here. She, uh—she kind of began making fun of me," I mumble, focusing on my hands shaping the pin. This is a conversation that I would really like to avoid. Luna sighs sadly, her old demeanor quickly returning.

"Kids. Still mean as ever, eh?" I stay quiet. I don't really want to talk about this, but I don't seem to have the guts to tell Luna that. Lucky for me, she senses my discomfort and leaves me be.

"I was seventeen when I got into the crash." I stop what I'm doing and look up. What did she say?

"I was driving myself to school on a normal day, and this car just came out of nowhere. The last thing I remember is praying that I would live long enough to graduate high school. I woke up in the hospital later that day; I'd never been more confused. Then I looked in the mirror. My right eye was gone, replaced with a crude glass prosthetic that looked more like a ball than an eye. I was partially blind." At this point, I stop trying to listen and work at the same time. It's obvious what Luna is doing: she's telling me her game origin story. Still, I can't hide my shock.

"We were a poorer family; that was the best prosthetic we could afford. Going back to school—oh, I'd never felt so humiliated before! I was the laughingstock of the school, and I was trying to adjust to life with partial sight." Sympathy floods my thoughts, but soon questions fight through. Is she still blind? I think back to when I first arrived in the game; I was so curious as to why Luna's right eye was so different from the left. It must have something to do with that accident.

"I was a stupid teenager, Ivy. Fitting in seemed like the most important thing in the world. I begged my parents to buy me the hot new video game—I thought maybe if I played the same game everyone else did, they would accept me." Luna paused to shake her head disapprovingly of her younger self's actions. "Despite our financial state, I got the game. I posted about it, talked about it whenever I could, but the bullying never stopped," she says softly.

"'Playing just to be liked' soon turned into 'playing to get out my frustration.' No matter what

I did, I was still an outcast. The more I bottled up my emotions, the more I played the game. It became life-consuming. Until one fateful day, I got trapped inside here." I nod. We all know that feeling.

"But when I landed here, I could see. I don't know how, or why, but The GameMaster gave me this." She points to her right eye—the bright blue color shining.

"If only we could go back and tell ourselves how stupid we were being, right?" Luna adds, her happy mood from our prior conversation returning. I smile and give her hand a firm squeeze of reassurance.

"Right."

A few minutes later, we finally perfect the key. I fist-bump Luna, who chuckles at the childish gesture. I haven't seen her this happy since I arrived in the game—and right after telling her origin story, too!

I walk up to Rory, makeshift key in hand, and hold it out with a smile. Ada and Sawyer push t past me and stuff their neatly written list into Rory's hand. He grins at us and grasps them both tightly. We all crowd around Rory, and enthusiastic murmurs spread. I cross my fingers as

Rory slides the "key" into the keyhole and turns it slightly. There is a small click, and we burst into (quiet) cheers. We did it!

The door creaks open and we all rush in, practically shoving each other out of the way. I stare in awe at the array of clothes and accessories in front of us. On the right are the more practical clothes: rows of cargo pants, leather shirts, combat boots, helmets, hats… It's a collection of stuff that could have made our lives a thousand times easier.

On the left side is the fun—but not necessarily useful—stuff. There are sparkly heels (running in those would be torture), fancy tops, jewelry, silly hats, and even fuzzy socks. I can't believe players actually made us wear those. It's a war zone, for pete's sake!

My instinct is to go straight for the protective armor, which is likely where most of the list's items are located, but everyone else is looking at the fun stuff, so against my better judgment, I join them.

"This would look amazing on Ada!" I joke, pulling a purple-and-orange feather boa from a rack. Rory snatches it out of my hand playfully, and drapes it around Ada's shoulders. She lets out a laugh. Mock-outraged, Sawyer suddenly crashes into us, nearly knocking me over.

"Purple and *orange*? Have I taught you nothing? That's hideous! Try this," he finishes with a smile, handing her a lei dotted with pink flowers.

"Oh, of course. Much better," I reply drily. Sawyer shoots me a grin. I find a matching blue-flowered lei and throw it to Rory, who chuckles before putting it on to coordinate with Ada. Sawyer finds me a rhinestone cowboy hat, which I wear with pride.

We end up putting Luna in a very retro-chic outfit complete with giant sunglasses and a rainbow purse. None of us can stop smiling.

"Bet you my breakfast that Rory won't wear these," Sawyer whispers into my ear, holding up a pair of neon-pink high heels. I smirk and accept the challenge. We shake hands to seal the deal and march up to Rory, who's now slow-dancing with Ada in the corner. I sigh. They are almost *too* perfect together.

"Hey, Rory!" we call in unison. Rory quickly moves away from Ada and blushes.

"Uh…yeah?" he replies, clearly suspicious.

"We hate to interrupt, but we think you would look great in these shoes!" I suggest. He gives me an annoyed look, but turns to face Ada. Her expression is curious and playfully challenging.

I watch with interest as he clearly weighs the dilemma in his head.

"Fine," he grumbles. I stick out my tongue at Sawyer's pouty face. By the time Rory manages to cram his feet into the tiny shoes, we're consumed with laughter.

"See? I can still walk—" He stumbles and nearly falls into the rest of us. Rory huffs, his stubborn nature taking hold. "I'm fine!" he insists as he wobbles around. "It's not that—*whoa*—"

To no one's surprise, he trips and collapses, bringing all of us down with him—and causing the loudest crash I've ever heard.

We are going to be in *so* much trouble.

Luckily, Luna and I end up being the ones who land on top of everyone else. We groan as we stand up, but are then faced with the heap of others tangled together. We share a worried glance.

As Luna and I begin helping everybody up, the faint sound of lights being turned on in another room startles us. Angry mumbling sounds in the hallway, and footsteps approach. There's only one person it could be.

"Crosby," I say with a wince. I help Ada to her feet. Sure enough, an annoyed-looking Crosby marches right past us before doing a double-take and entering the wardrobe. His eyes widen when he realizes what we're doing.

"What—how—why—" he shouts, struggling to find the right words for his anger. Sawyer walks over and puts his arm around Crosby's shoulder. Crosby stiffens and glares at him.

"Oh, relax! It's not *that* big of a deal," Sawyer attempts to reason. Crosby shoots him another glare, and I stifle a laugh at his attitude. Sawyer walks away, playfully mocking Crosby's angry demeanor.

Crosby, now fully awakened from his drowsy, confused state, finally decides on "You're *playing dress-up* in the middle of the night!"

"He's not wrong…," Sawyer whispers to me. I giggle and pass the joke on to Ada. She snorts with laughter.

"How did you even get in here?" Crosby asks. Even if he is fuming, it's apparent that he's also quite curious how we, of all people, found our way inside. A smug expression spreads across Rory's face as he steps forward.

"Me!" he declares proudly. Annoyed by his cockiness, Ada tugs on the back of his shirt and drags him backwards to stand next to her again.

"Wait a minute there. *You* came up with the plan. *We* actually did it," she reminds him, pointing an accusatory finger at his face.

"I did make the plan, so technically—" Rory begins stubbornly.

"I don't give a crap how you got in here," Crosby interrupts, contradicting himself in his indignation. Rory pretends to be offended. "The real question is *why*?" Crosby ends, obviously desperate for some explanation. I butt in this time.

"Well, we were supposed to be gathering protective armor for the escape, but things got a little out of hand." I laugh quietly as the image of Rory wobbling around in pink high heels resurfaces in my mind. "We'll grab the stuff we need and leave as soon as possible!" I assure him. "I think we could all use the sleep." The four heads nodding vigorously back me up. Crosby crosses his arms and rolls his eyes, but obliges.

"Grab some stuff for me too," Crosby calls through a yawn as he leaves. We all heave a sigh of relief when he finally exits. In a more serious mindset, we neatly replace all of our fun outfits and go on a search for the more practical items that made their way onto our list. After a bit of looking, I decide on a pair of camo pants, a white tank top, a black leather jacket, and black boots. It's a lot more protective than my current outfit (which I've been wearing for a few months, thanks to a player's purchase). I grab a few additional throwing knives and a pistol to have on hand as weapons during the escape. I've gotten pretty good at the art of knife-throwing in my two years of living the game, but you never know when you're going to need something a bit more…well, lethal.

Ada picks out black leggings, a leather crop top, and knee-high boots. She also finds a new sword (she is deadly with any long blade). Rory chooses some thick black pants and a camo jacket to go with his enormous rifle, and Luna selects a simple black jumpsuit made from a thick synthetic fabric and a set of spears. Unsurprisingly, Sawyer takes ages to find his outfit, but eventually settles on a black long-sleeved shirt, black jeans, a brown belt, and these cool, dark distressed suspenders. The ensemble suits his weapon choice of sturdy bow and arrow to a T. It gives me post-apocalypse vibes.

I grab outfits for Juniper and a few of the second-shift people while Rory finds something for Crosby and the rest of the second shift. Once everyone has what they need, we lock up the closet—Luna keeps the key in case we need it again—and head to bed. Before I drift into sleep, I lay out my outfit on my nightstand and put my weapons in the drawer with the utmost care. I worked hard to get them—I'm going to make sure they are as safe as possible. We are one step closer to escaping.

I can't believe it. I am going to get out of here.

CHAPTER 12

1 WEEK UNTIL ESCAPE

"Sewing? I can't sew!" Rory exclaims as I reveal the pile of cloth on the ground. I sigh, annoyed.

"Well, good thing the world doesn't revolve around you!" Ada teases, gesturing to herself and Luna, Crosby, and Sawyer standing next to her. Rory narrows his eyes and opens his mouth to retort, but I stop him.

"Guys! There's no time to argue. We need to make these bags today or we won't have enough time to organize the rest of the materials before the escape!" I half-remind, half-warn them. I'm a fan of their mock-arguments every now and then, but we really need to focus right now. Ada and Rory both sigh and agree to stop their playful fighting—for now.

Juniper is working hard in the control room to finalize the virus before the big day. For the past few weeks, we've all been making sure we have everything we need prepared for the escape. We've saved up rations, collected water bottles, "borrowed" weapons, etc. But there's one thing we are still missing: bags.

When we do runs, our outfits always have pockets to store our weapons and a bottle of water. We've never needed anything bigger to carry items. For the escape, though, it will be impossible to carry all our supplies through the treacherous terrain that Juniper claims we'll encounter. We thought about cleaning the containers our food comes in and using those, but they are too small for everything we need. We even scrounged around the closet during our little break in, but we came out empty handed. Our only option is to make our own bags.

Luna is an expert at sewing, so she takes the lead on this one. We have carved small needles out of the wood chips from a chair in the common room (that chair is ancient) and gotten thread by meticulously pulling apart frayed fabric. While we were raiding the closet a few weeks ago, Luna grabbed a few simple cotton shirts and pants, thinking that we would probably find them useful. Thanks to her intuition, we now have the fabric necessary for the bags.

I've spent the last hour attempting to tear the clothing into even pieces of fabric. They're anything *but* even, but they'll do the job. I distribute the crudely torn pieces of fabric, making sure that everyone has enough for a bag.

"Okay, who has the list?" I ask, scanning the others' faces.

"I do!" Ada chirps, pulling a crumpled piece of paper from her pocket. She attempts to smooth it out for a couple seconds, but eventually gives up.

"We need one for each of us, so that's six— plus Juniper, that's seven." I keep a mental note of her numbers in my head to compare to the amount of fabric we have. "The second-shifters are Jaclyn, Corinne, Tony, and Ron. That's four more bags. We need eleven total. Got it?" she finishes, stuffing the list back into her pocket. I thank her with a smile.

I glance at Luna, who shakes her head regretfully. My smile turns into a frown as I smack my palm to my forehead and groan.

"We're one short!" I exclaim, frustrated. Rory's eyes meet Ada's.

"It's fine! We can share!" he says with a smile, as Ada gives him a small squeeze. Crosby groans.

"Give me a break!" he complains, crossing his arms. I laugh.

Luna takes over and begins teaching us how to sew. She is quite good at it, but Sawyer drops a few helpful hints every so often. The instructions are pretty clear, but most of us are new to sewing, so some of our bags are bound to look better than others. Thankfully, Luna understands that and moves slowly so that everyone can keep up. Nonetheless, by the time we're almost done, all of our bags look worlds different.

Sawyer's looks like he went out and bought it from a fancy store. Obviously Luna's is perfect, and Crosby's is surprisingly decent. I struggle a bit, but not as much as Ada and Rory do. The "bags" they are working on just look like giant balls of fabric, but honestly, what were we expecting from them? I'm pretty sure they ended up bribing Sawyer to do theirs. Still, we're having more fun than ever.

"This reminds me of this story I have," Sawyer starts. We all glance around in confusion.

"Um…what reminds you of the story?" Rory asks. Sawyer gestures to our bags—which are in worse shape than ever—and we chuckle before he continues.

"One time, I went camping to look for inspiration—" Sawyer begins casually, but we cut him off almost immediately.

"You went...*camping*?" Ada exclaims as she bursts out laughing. I can't help but join her; I'm laughing so hard I have to put down my half-sewn bag. He sticks his tongue out at both of us and we try to suppress our giggles long enough for him to finish his story.

"As I was *saying*," he says emphatically, giving me and Ada a pointed glare. I snicker. "It was just a sort of inspirational trip, you know? I wanted to come up with designs that were nature inspired, and I couldn't really do that from the polluted streets of L.A. I remember that I got so inspired that I- I—" Sawyer pauses to chuckle lightly. "I made a dress out of leaves. While I was making it I thought it was the cutest thing on earth. And then I came home and realized it looked like a literal pile of trash—just like *your* bag, Ada!" he adds playfully, earning a light punch on the arm from Ada. I giggle at their play-fight.

Honestly, I would give anything to be in nature again. Camping was one of my favorite activities to do with my family—but every year, Jane and I would go camping, and I can't help but think back to the happy times we spent together.

Everything was so…relaxing, and carefree, and…

Simple.

"Race you to our spot!" Jane exclaimed, hauling all of her bags over her shoulder and sprinting towards our camp site.

"Hey! Wait up!" I exclaim, trying to catch up with her.

Our eighth grade year had come to a close, and we were starting off the summer with our annual camping trip. Except, this time it was very different. Thanks to a lot of convincing from me and Jane, our parents had finally agreed to let us go on the trip alone. There were no parents! Just me, Jane, and the great outdoors. Naturally, we were pumped. We had big plans for our night!

"Jane! I suck at this!" I gestured to the collapsed tent that I had been attempting to set up. She glanced at me and chuckled at my distress.

"Fine—you can cook dinner," she said, shoving two hot dogs and a handful of sticks into my hand. Jane knew that I'm a terrible cook! I moped over to the fire and caught Jane giving me an amused expression.

"Ow!" she screeched as one of my sticks collided with her arm. I gave her the most innocent smile

I could muster up and we both laughed. This was going to be fun.

The rest of the evening was a blast! I actually didn't burn dinner, we shared the latest gossip with each other, and Jane got the tent up and habitable. We ran around exploring the area for hours on end until the sun finally began setting and we were forced to make our way back. After sharing some spooky ghost stories by the fire, we made our way inside our tent and started setting up our "beds" for the night. There was only one problem.

"Jane? You brought the blankets and pillows, right?" I asked nervously as my rummaging through my bag intensified. Even though it was the beginning of summer, the slight chill in the air had us shivering. Jane shook her head.

"I thought you *were going to bring them!" I smacked my forehead. Great! Now we didn't have anything to sleep on.*

"What do we do now?" I groaned, my discomfort obvious as I lay down on the hard floor of the tent. Of course, with my clumsiness, I managed to hit my head on a rock.

Jane was deep in thought; I could see all of the options running through her brain until she snapped her fingers. "I've got it!"

Jane grabbed my hand and used the flashlight beam to lead us out of the tent and into the pitch-black darkness. What was she up to? I kept a tight grip on her hand as we moved from our tent towards the large group of bushes in the corner. There was a small strip of mud next to the bushes from some rain earlier. I gave Jane a questioning look and she smiled proudly as if it was obvious what we were doing.

"Um...so why exactly are we here?" I asked bluntly (because apparently my dumbfounded expression wasn't hint enough).

"Come on, silly! Leaves plus mud equals a blanket and pillows!" Jane whispered. I paused, unsure I had heard her correctly.

"I- what?" "Just trust me, okay?" she said, beginning to pick leaves from the bushes. Even though I knew this was the stupidest idea that Jane had ever had, and I'm sure she knew too, I played along for the fun of it.

As we plucked leaves and scooped up mud, Jane refused to stop cracking dumb jokes despite the million times that I told her to stop. So, there we were, gathering leaves and mud in the middle of the night and laughing our heads off.

"Hurry up! It's cold!" Jane whined loudly, nodding towards the enormous glob of mud sitting in her hands.

I shook my head disapprovingly and quickly hurried back toward our tent with my pile of leaves. I couldn't help but laugh as Jane's mud began dripping all over her on our way back. She ended up sprinting back and practically throwing the glob on the floor of our tent. Once I caught up, I was heaving with laughter at her expression and the huge mess that she'd made, but Jane simply refused to give up on her idea.

"Look! It's going to work! We just take this…" She grabbed a few of my leaves and slathered mud over them. I cringed at the uncomfortable squelching sound and she rolled her eyes at me. According to Jane, this wasn't gross—it was the beauty of nature! "And now we repeat that…Are you going to help me or not?" Jane exclaimed, poking at me with her muddy finger. After a bit of complaining, I finally obliged and joined her.

It took almost an hour of sticking leaves together in order to form the crude outline of a blanket. Of course, we couldn't do all of that work in complete silence. We made up a guessing game that involved our favorite songs, my obnoxious humming, and lots of laughs. By the time the "blanket" was almost finished, we weren't even a tiny bit bored.

"Now what?" I asked as I carefully smoothed out our hard work. Jane looked up at me without a response, and I waved my hand in front of her face.

"Hello? Earth to Jane!" Jane snapped out of her daze. "Well, what do we do now? How are we supposed to make the mud dry so that we can finally get some sleep?"

"Uh...I don't know. To be honest, I didn't really think this far," Jane admitted sheepishly. My jaw dropped and she gave me an innocent-looking smile. While keeping my eyes completely trained on Jane, I slowly dipped my hand into our giant pile of extra mud and got a big scoop of it. She eyed my surreptitious movements and began inching away from me, her devilish smile unwavering.

"You really didn't think it through, huh? You didn't just make me do all of that work for no reason?" I asked with narrowed eyes. She shrugged her shoulders and winked at me, but continued to play innocent.

"Little Miss Smarty-Pants really forgot about something that simple? Wow, I guess you aren't such a genius after all," I teased, and she burst out laughing. I made my way closer to Jane, mud in hand.

"Well, if you didn't mean to do that...then I guess I didn't mean to do that either!" I yelled, thrusting the sticky mud onto Jane's face. I immediately burst into a fit of laughter, the image of her surprised face running through my head over and over. I really got her good! Just as I was getting my giggling under *control, something cold and slimy landed on my face. I yelped in surprise. I wiped the mud from my forehead to find Jane staring at me with more mud in her hands and a mischievous glimmer in her eyes.*

"Oh, it is on*!" she exclaimed.*

It's safe to say that we got absolutely no sleep that night, and it was by far the messiest camping trip ever, but I still smile whenever I remember what was the best trip of our lives.

"Ivy? Is that a yes?" Luna's familiar voice lurches me back to reality and I look at her in confusion, trying to shake the flashback out of my head. I guess Luna of all people understands spacing out from time to time.

"I asked if you were done with your bag," she repeated.

"Oh, yeah, I am. Well, if this can even be called a bag," I reply jokingly, looking down at the messily sewn piece of fabric in front of me. My mind can't help but drift back to our mud-blanket as I stare at it. How I miss those days.

Sawyer nudges me and points to Ada and Rory's even worse bag as consolation, and I laugh, falling back into a conversation with the group.

We've been having these group activities after our shift more and more frequently as the day of the escape approaches, but they're always so serious. Sometimes planning, sometimes prepping, but never that much fun. This time, we all had a blast, even if some of our bags didn't turn out too well.

It really makes me appreciate the people that I have grown to think of as family over the past two years. In a few days, we'll go our separate ways. We'll all go back to our normal lives as normal people. We won't ever get to spend time like this again. We'll talk and hang out, of course, but it won't be the same. It makes me a little sad to think about that, but I know that I now have six friends for life.

CHAPTER 13

12 HOURS UNTIL ESCAPE

"Hey, can I talk to you?" Ada asks. She seems tense. We all are stressed about the big day, but Ada seems extra worried.

"Sure!" I mumble, my mouth still full with the last few bites of cauliflower from dinner. I deposit my dishes in the trash, grab a bottle of water, and follow Ada back to her room. She shuts the door and leads me to a chair. We sit down, and silence follows for the next few seconds.

"Um…is everything all right?" I ask nervously as I unscrew the cap of my bottle. Ada is usually either making some sarcastic remark or gushing about Rory. It is totally unlike her to be *quiet* and *awkward*. I'm pretty sure those words and "Ada" have never been in the same sentence together before.

Ada nods. She chews on her lip and takes a quick breath before explaining.

"Everything is great! That's the thing. I haven't told anyone this yet. Not even Rory," she says. A lock of hair obscures her eyes, and I brush it out of the way.

"Wow! If Rory doesn't know, I must *really* be special!" I say playfully before taking a sip of water. Ada rolls her eyes and punches my arm good-naturedly. I'm being sarcastic, but I'm still concerned as to why she is acting this way.

"Okay, stop! Seriously. I think…well, er— I think that…" Ada stutters. My worry isn't going anywhere; this sounds serious.

"What? Ada, just tell me!" I beg, my joking attitude falling away. I can't stand so much tension.

"Okay, okay! Well…I think that I'm…I'm… *pregnant!*" she blurts.

I spew a mouthful of water all over myself in shock. After almost choking on what remains of the water, I finally began processing what Ada has told me. She's pregnant. My best friend— she's *pregnant.* And I couldn't be more thrilled for her. I cannot believe that *my* Ada is going to be a mom; it's the best news I've heard in years.

I leap out of my chair and envelop Ada in a hug. I practically knock her over in my excitement.

I'm *so* thrilled, in fact, that I don't even realize that I am soaking wet. I think that's irrelevant, but Ada forces me to clean myself up a little before she will tell me any more. Once I have retrieved a towel from the bathroom and dried myself off as best I can, she continues.

"Okay—relax a little!" she says, failing to conceal her huge grin. She pauses for a second, I assume to try to organize her thoughts in a semi-put-together way. If I'm totally going bezerk, I can't even begin to imagine how *she's* feeling at the moment!

"I want him to grow up free, and now that we might actually…well, you know, it's just—" I stop her before she can even finish her sentence. I understand exactly what she means. This—what we had to go through—I wouldn't wish it on anybody. Now that we have a chance to get out of here…Ada is going to get to *live*. We are all going to live real lives and be happy and free, and this is Ada's idea of being happy: starting a family with the man she loves. *This* is Ada's happily ever after.

She wraps her arms around her stomach protectively. I grin.

"Him?" I tease. Her eyes widen.

"Oh! I didn't even realize I said that. Mother's instinct, I guess," she replies playfully. We giggle and I shake my head slowly. It still feels unreal. My Ada—a mom! Before she can say anything else, I encourage her to go tell Rory. The man is going to be a dad, for pete's sake!

When we leave Ada's room, Rory is standing right outside, arms crossed and eyes narrowed. He definitely knows something is up. I make some extremely awkward excuse to give Ada privacy to tell him and quickly leave the area. I'm sure he is going to be so excited! I already know Rory is going to be an amazing dad.

What's taking them so long? I thought Ada would want to get it out quickly. Well, maybe she needs a little time.

I take a seat on a sofa in the living area, waiting patiently as the time ticks by. The others give me curious looks as they pass by, and despite my urge to blurt out the good news, I know I have to wait. By the time ten minutes have passed, I can't take it anymore. I tiptoe back towards Ada's bedroom and carefully lean against the door. That's odd—it's silent. I gulp. That can't be good. A slightly muffled voice begins to speak, and I press my ear harder against the door.

"I'm sorry, Ada, I just—I can't do this right now," Rory says gruffly. I clap my hand over my mouth. That is *not* the way I expected him to react—I was positive that he would be jumping up and down in excitement. I hear his footsteps coming towards the door, and I jump backwards, scrambling to get away from it. Rory opens it quietly and avoids my eye; he races to his room and slams the door. Immediately, I run into the room and rush to Ada to give her a big hug. Her face is red and tearstained and I see her hunched over in the corner.

"Oh my gosh, Ada, come here!" I exclaim, wrapping my arms around her in a comforting gesture. Instead of melting into my arms, she stiffens and I pause.

"Go away. Please. I have to be alone right now." I step backwards, stumbling over an apology, but Ada remains silent. I stay by the door for a few seconds in case she wants to call me back, but I can tell there's little hope of that.

I feel terrible for her. Just minutes ago we were laughing and smiling about it. I'm completely thrilled by the news. But when it comes to the actual father of the baby, he's not happy? Not to mention he left her in there crying... Why would Rory do this to Ada?

This situation doesn't make sense to me. There has to be something I'm missing. Against my better judgement, I decide to take matters into my own hands. Cautiously, I creak open the door to Rory's room to find him sitting on his bed with his head in his hands.

"Who told you you could come in?" he sighs in frustration. I quietly shut the door behind me and take a seat next to Rory. We both know that I am not going to listen to him no matter how many times he tells me to leave.

"I thought you could use someone to talk to," I respond quietly. Rory relaxes a little. That's an improvement, at least.

"Why did you *say* that? You know Ada. You know how much courage it took for her to tell you; I practically had to force her to go do it." Rory stays quiet for a few seconds.

"I- I can't be a *father*!" he exclaims in exasperation, throwing his hands in the air. I glance up at him.

"I can't raise a child! I'm just a dumb quarterback who has been stuck in a video game, away from the real world, for practically a decade and happened to fall in love. Of course I want to have a baby, but how am I supposed to raise a child? I know nothing about how to take care of a baby; I'd be a terrible father. And what about Ada? How is she going to react when she realizes how useless I am? I won't be able to care for them the way they need me to! They're probably better off without me," Rory finishes glumly. I stare at him blankly.

And then I smack him upside the head. Not hard, just enough to get my point across and bring him back to his senses.

"Ow!" He rubs his tender head.

"Please tell me you didn't just say that," I whisper with disgust. Rory cocks his head at me in confusion.

"Rory, you would be a *great* father. You're kind, you're hilarious, and it's obvious you would do anything for Ada! You can't expect to immediately be a perfect dad, though; you have to work for it. And I can't believe how selfish you're being! You haven't stopped to think how Ada is feeling right now. *She* doesn't have any choice in this! Whether you feel ready or not, Ada needs you! You can do this, Rory. You're going to be amazing parents. Now shut up and go apologize to her," I end on a less serious note. Rory looks a lot less stressed; he even cracks a tiny smile. Maybe I should consider a career as a relationship counselor after all.

"You really think so?" he asks hopefully. I nod. Everything I said was 100% true.

"Thank you, Ivy. I don't know what I would do without you." I wink and remind him to go talk to Ada. He gives me one last grateful smile and rushes out of the room.

I slowly make my way back to the living area and wait on the couch. If his apology goes well, they should be out soon. In the meantime, I busy myself playing cards with Luna and Sawyer.

Sure enough, about fifteen minutes later, Ada and Rory slowly make their way into the living area, hand in hand. Ada's face is much less red and she wears a small smile on her face to complement Rory's wide grin. She leans over to me to whisper something.

"Turns out he was just worried that he wouldn't be a good father!" she says, clearly in a much better mood. I grin eagerly and give her a thumbs-up. Thank goodness! Ada and Rory soon make their way all around to all of the others to make the big announcement.

Naturally, everyone is ecstatic—no one more than me, though. I know how happy this is going to make them, and seeing my friends smile means everything to me. The new addition to our group makes everyone even more determined for the escape to succeed. The life of this child depends on it, so we can't screw this up.

We can't celebrate for long, though, because our escape is in less than twelve hours. If we are going to survive, we have to pause the celebration for now and continue our preparations for the big day.

"Okay, so we have backpacks," I read from our checklist of things to bring. Rory hoists ten freshly sewn bags into the air. I nod approvingly, and place a large check mark in the appropriate box.

"And...water stash?" Ada gives me a thumbs-up and gestures to a pile of unopened bottles.

"Good. Now, extra food?"

I go down the list, making sure we're as prepared as possible. Each one of us is supposed to have a few meals, a big bottle of water, weapons, a change of clothes, a handkerchief, and a few "miracle pills." Once all of the boxes are checked off and I've double-checked the list, I dismiss everyone to pack their backpacks with the supplies we have gathered. Something is nagging at me, though.

"Hey, Sawyer?" I plop down next to him as he neatly organizes his belongings in the bag.

"What's up?" he asks, keeping his eyes glued to the task at hand. I shuffle uncomfortably.

"Nothing…Well…I feel like this has been too easy, you know? If no one has escaped since Luna's group, then why is it that, all of a sudden, we figure out a way to get out?" I blurt out. He pauses and glances at me, trying to read my facial expression. I'm a little shocked at my outburst myself. I didn't really know that's what I felt until I said it.

"Look, maybe you're overthinking this. Like you said, Luna's cohort did escape. We know it's possible," he replies, trying to reason with me.

"But that was before—" I begin, frustrated.

"Let's stick to the plan, okay?" he interrupts. "You just need to relax. We're all stressed, and it's natural to have second thoughts." I nod, a feeble attempt to convince myself that he is right. Why am I trying to talk myself *out* of escaping?

"Here," Sawyer says. He hands me my bag and gestures towards our little "goodie bar." I sigh. Maybe I *am* overthinking it. Tomorrow is what we've been working towards for months; I'm probably just nervous. I shrug it off and get in line for the goodie bar.

Looking over the supplies we have gathered, I'm really proud. In one month, we have managed to collect everything we need—and even made our own bags to carry it all! We may seem like we're all fun and games, but when our lives are on the line, the group gets the job done. I quickly grab items and stuff them into my pack, which already seems to be falling apart at the seams. I'll have to restitch those parts later tonight, I guess. I've never really been that good at sewing. From the time I was little, I tried but I could never get it right. That never stopped my mom from trying to teach me, though.

"Moooom! Do I have to?" I moaned as I dragged my feet. She gave me a gentle smile and kneeled down next to me. Her gray-green eyes stared into mine, kindness radiating from them. She leaned in and softly kissed my forehead before taking my hand in hers and leading me to the sewing machine. I cocked my head curiously at seeing the large metal device sitting before me. My mother laughed at my dumbfounded expression and started to explain the process.

Her delicate hands worked perfectly in sync with the machine. I sat down and simply stared, completely captivated at how easily she did it. I was mesmerized. My mother's relaxing voice patiently guided me through the steps.

Minutes later, she had two beautiful fleece mittens. It was incredible! My reluctance suddenly turned into eagerness. I couldn't wait to try it!

Thread here, needle here, fabric there—it couldn't be that difficult, right? I eagerly grabbed a bright yellow piece of cloth and started to copy my mother's actions. I couldn't remember all of them exactly, but figured if I had the general idea that should be enough.

She tried to help me a little, but I refused to let her do it for me. I was going to do this all on my own. I was doing the same things my mom did, but hers looked so much better than mine! What could I be doing wrong?

Despite my doubts, I did not accept my mom's offer to help and kept doing what I was doing. If I just kept working at it, it was bound to turn out well. Or at least that's what I told myself.

Twenty minutes later, I was lying on the floor crying while tangled in thread and holding two mismatched mittens. I wailed for my mom, who came sprinting from the restroom, straight to my aid. She scooped me up and soothed my tears with a big hug.

I sobbed quietly into her warm sweater, burying my head into her chest. She shushed me kindly, rocking me back and forth in her motherly embrace. My tears slowed after a little while, and soon stopped.

A few minutes after my meltdown, my mother slowly began unraveling the mess of thread I was stuck in. She ended up making it a game, and by the time the last piece of thread was off me, I was almost smiling.

She grabbed my mittens and raced upstairs. Soon afterwards, she returned with a perfect pair of sunny yellow mittens to replace the ones that I'd attempted to make. Then, she took my hand and led me to the family room. On the couch sat two big fluffy blankets, two cups of hot cocoa, and my favorite Christmas movie. Jane stood by the door, all bundled up with a slight smile on her face. She shot me a shy wave. My frown slowly turned into a smile.

"Hey! Juniper wants to show us our escape route for tomorrow. You coming?" Rory nudges me, pointing to the small group gathering a couple feet away from me. I nod enthusiastically and hurry to join them before anything big happens. I nestle myself next to Ada, who seems to brighten when I arrive.

"All right. I know we discussed the general plan a few months ago, but now I have it all figured out in much more detail, so pay attention please! This is it," Juniper starts. I nod, focusing all my attention on her and the map.

"We start early in the morning—as soon as the second shift ends, I release the virus. The programmers will notice it and shut down the game for a little while to fix it, so we don't have to worry about missing our shift. Then, we all gather together and climb up the drop chute. Each of you should have two knives for that. It's going to be a *long* climb, so be prepared. At the top, we should reach a long series of hallways. I'm talking multiple miles here. There will be some obstacles and traps to try and outsmart us, but we'll be prepared for them. The portal should be at the very end, and that's pretty much it. I don't foresee any huge issues, but whatever happens, we can work it out!" As she finishes up, she traces the route on the map with her finger, and we all thank her.

Juniper's plan is everything we could have asked for: clear, organized, and simple. Not one person isn't satisfied with it. To my surprise, Juniper slides it—the map to our freedom!—into my bag. *Me*, of all people. Why couldn't she have chosen Sawyer? At least he is good at organization. I'm sure I'll lose it. Nonetheless, I carefully place my bag right next to my bed, checking every ten minutes to make sure the map is still accounted for.

Dinner is tense. We know that as soon as we wake up, Juniper will activate and release the virus—for real this time. We evenly ration out six meals, saving one for the last meal that we need tomorrow. Luna grabs the saved-up meal and places it in her bag. Now, each of us has two meals and a snack for the big day.

Everyone eats quickly and heads for bed as soon as they can. Or at least they try to.

"Wait! Everyone, come back!" Sawyer shouts desperately from the living-room area. I share a bemused glance with the others before turning around to meet his gaze.

"What now, Sawyer?" Crosby asks, annoyed. For once, I'm with him. I thought we were supposed to go to bed early tonight!

"I know we're all really stressed out—for a lot of different reasons—but I think that we should lighten the mood a little. You know, to make it easier for everyone to get enough sleep," Well, that didn't clear up anything.

"And how do you suggest we do that?" I reply. Sawyer smiles.

"Why don't we share what we are looking forward to getting back to? As a real-world transition activity…thing," he suggests. Huh. . I almost forgot about that part of our escape: we're going to be back in the real world! I've been so focused on the plan and trying not to die that what happens *after* we escape sort of slipped my mind. I can't believe that after all this time, we're going to have to integrate back into society, return to work and school, and—well, maybe Sawyer's idea isn't a bad one. We all agree and take our seats again.

Sawyer says, "I guess since I proposed this whole idea, I might as well go first! I can't wait to get back to my studio. Sure, the first couple weeks were a nice break from working, but after that, it became torture. I don't even care if no one buys my stuff, I just want to get back to designing. It's my passion! And, man, do I miss it." We all nod in understanding. I can't imagine how he's gone all these years without it.

"Do you design maternity clothes?" Ada jokes.

"For you? Of course."

After an annoying argument about who should go next, Crosby snaps, "I'll do it! Would you all just shut up? I thought this was supposed to make us calmer!" Immediately we hush our bickering. Thank goodness—I have no idea how to choose what I want to go back to yet, and I had been sure everyone was ready to pick me.

"I can't wait to get back to Thai food," Crosby states plainly. I snort. He glares at me. I blink.

"Wha—you're being serious?" I blurt. Almost everyone rolls their eyes at me.

"Does it look like I'm joking?" he asks, hardening his gaze. I resist the urge to laugh. Thai food? Really? "We've had every other type of cuisine here. Italian, French, Indian, Chinese—you name it! But never in twenty-five years has any Thai food come through that food chute. And that just so happens to be my favorite food. That's the first thing I'm going to do when we get home: get some Thai food." Crosby sees my skeptical look and rolls his eyes again.

"Cut me some slack! Aren't we supposed to be honest? Plus, it's not like you've said anything yet," Crosby says. I shrug—fair enough, I guess. Luna offers to go next, saving us from another unnecessary argument.

"I- I don't have a very good memory of what the real world is like, but I do know one thing that I can't wait to get back to." We perk up in curiosity.

"Nature. I miss it more every day. I used to sit for hours taking in the view. Oh, what it would be like to see a real tree again! Or even some flowers.

I played outside all throughout my childhood; it's a part of me," Luna murmurs. She's right—I can't believe I haven't seen nature in almost two years. Nature used to be such a huge part of my life, and this place has almost completely wiped it from my mind. I wonder what else I've forgotten about.

It's quiet for a couple of seconds, undoubtedly due to a lack of volunteers to share next.

"Ada?" I say, breaking the silence. Reluctantly, she obliges.

"Okay, so I can't wait to go back to *the world*. I know that sounds really vague. I used to travel so much; I would never get bored because there was so much to see! I've been trapped inside this *box* for way too long. I want to explore again!" Ada gushes. That's a pretty good one. I haven't gotten to travel much, and there are so many places I've dreamed about visiting. I wonder what it's going to be like to see a real, bustling city again instead of the ruins I see while doing runs in the game.

"Your turn, Ivy!" Ada exclaims fake-sweetly. I cringe. I don't want to go next! I turn towards Rory and give him the most innocent look I can muster up. He rolls his eyes and grumbles. I flash him a smile.

"Ugh. Fine! I really want to go home to…well, my home. It's not just my house, though. It's my family, my friends, all of the memories I made there. I lived there my whole life, you know? Never moved once. When I first got here, I was homesick for weeks. I can't wait to finally be back home again," Rory admits. Ada gives him a tight hug and he grins. I shake my head. I guess we all know where those two are going to settle down after the escape.

"Well, Ivy?" I jerk up. "I covered for you. It's your turn now!" Rory reminds me. I sigh. At least I have an idea what to say now.

"Okay, okay. For me, I want to get back to my family. They're the best. We were all so close, and I miss them. No matter what I did or how much I pretended to hate them, they were always there for me. It sounds cliche—trust me, I know—but I'm being serious. I really miss them. Especially my little brother," I state sheepishly. It really is true. Although I pushed them away the last few weeks before I got transferred here, I had such an amazing relationship with them. We would spend weekends together and tease each other. The saddest part is that I didn't even realize how much that closeness meant to me until I lost it. I know things will never be quite the same, but I hope we can have that again. If I can even regain even a fraction of what our bond used to be, I'll be happy.

Everyone gives me slight nods and understanding smiles, which makes me feel a little better.

"Juniper, you're the last one," Sawyer says. I cheer silently. Sleep, here I come! However, Juniper fidgets uncomfortably and stays silent. I give her a gentle nudge, but she remains frozen.

"Juniper—" I begin.

"I don't have anything that I want to go home to." I narrow my eyes. There's no way there's nothing she misses. Of all of us, Juniper has been here for the shortest amount of time! If anything, she should be the one with the most to go back to.

"Whaaat? Come on, everyone has *something*—"

"Well, I don't! So could you just stop asking me?" Juniper snaps.

It's dead silent. Even Crosby doesn't sound that mean when he snaps! Her expression immediately softens and she apologizes, but everyone leaves her alone and heads to bed.

Everyone except for me, that is. Juniper has certainly had her bad days, but she has never acted like this before. I need to make sure that she is in the right mindset for the escape tomorrow.

"Hey, Juniper? You in there?" I say quietly, rapping my knuckles on her bedroom door. I hear a familiar heavy sigh and open the door. Juniper is sprawled across her bed with a pillow covering her face.

I know stress when I see it. "Tell me what's up." She slowly removes the pillow and sits up. As much as she tries to hide it, I can see that her eyes are puffy and red from crying. She shuffles around uncomfortably before settling down enough to talk.

"I- I don't know what that was. It's the stress, Ivy! I can't deal with it. All of your lives are in my hands, and if I fail, everyone dies and it will be my fault. How am I supposed to—I can't even—" Juniper throws her hands over her face in despair.

I let her calm down for a couple seconds before putting my arm around her.

"Hey, don't stress out! We are all going to make it—and even if something happens, no one is going to blame you." Juniper looks up and gives me a slight smile. That's more like the Juniper I know! Her expression changes into a look of deep thought, and she hesitates.

"Um...Ivy? Can I tell you something?" she blurts out. I immediately nod. She can always tell me anything!

"I—uh—never mind," Juniper backpedals awkwardly. I give her a curious look but shrug it off.

"Thank you for checking up on me. I really needed that," she admits.

"Any time!" I say, giving her hand a tight squeeze.

Not long afterwards, we dismiss ourselves to bed (despite the still-early time.) Although we plan to get to sleep as early as possible to maximize our energy, we all know that no one will be sleeping much tonight (despite Sawyer's efforts.) Especially not me. There are so many things that can go wrong. But the thing that really keeps me up is that Sawyer's suggestion made me think about seeing my family again. That scares me more than the thought of a perilous escape. How can I face them after years away? Will they even recognize me?

I don't mean in a physical way; I look pretty much the way I did when I first arrived here. But personality-wise...my two years here have changed me so much. I'm not the moody high-schooler that I was. I've matured! And I don't have the silly personality that my old self did—the one that my family knew. So many questions cloud my brain, but I attempt to push them away. I really need to be well rested for tomorrow!

As I predicted, I get about half an hour of sleep that night; my brain is too busy whizzing with thoughts of freedom. Judging from the amount of rustling, tossing, and turning I hear, I assume that few of us get any sleep at all. But we can't let a lack of sleep derail our plans. We've been waiting for this day for years, decades, even. This is our chance. Our one chance to be free.

CHAPTER 14

My alarm beeps loudly, but I'm already wide awake. I hop out of bed and dress in the protective clothes set neatly on my nightstand. A small smile plays on my lips as I reminisce about our closet break-in a month ago. I'll have to cherish those memories for as long as I can. Swinging my bag over my shoulder, I close the door to a chapter of my life with a smile on my face. This is one chapter that I am happy to say goodbye to.

My assumption last night was correct: it looks as if there are six zombies swarming the kitchen. Although they're more expectant than your average zombies. I wave hello to Ada and immediately notice that Juniper doesn't look good. She is pale and shivering profusely. I place a hand on her shoulder; the comforting gesture seems to relax her a bit. She looks at me with a grateful smile, but it's as if she is using that to hide another emotion that I can't put a finger on. It's probably nothing. It makes sense that she's nervous! We all are.

Breakfast is very rushed, the kitchen quiet. I stuff down my food in seconds and chug my coffee. We have a schedule to uphold! I finish before everyone else, so I decide to take one last look at our living quarters, where I've spent every second of the last two years.

I smile slightly as I run my hand across the couch where I sit for meals. I try to remember all of the crazy conversations that we've had while I was sitting there, and I chuckle at the silly memories. My handmade set of playing cards sits on the table in the center of the room. I stare at them for a few seconds. I've probably played with those hundreds of times.

I glance around to make sure no one is looking before quickly sliding a single card into my pocket. I want a token of my stay here. As much as I'd love to forget most of my time here, I know that there are some parts of it that I'd like to treasure for as long as I can. These cards are a reminder of all the good times I've spent with the people I now call family.

My eyes graze over the kitchen and food chute. Snippets of us laughing and joking there flash in my head. I almost tear up. That's the one and only thing I am going to miss from this whole experience: my best friends.

Before I can get too sentimental, Rory calls me over to signal that everyone is ready to initiate the plan. I nod and follow the group down the hallway. Right before we enter the control room, Juniper suggests that we check our supplies again.

We run through the list twice and confirm that we have everything we need. Even though it's a simple action, it calms my nerves—at least I know that we won't be going hungry or dying of thirst.

Crosby opens the door to the control room and gestures for us to enter. This is it.

We all squeeze into the control room and wait quietly. Juniper's watch makes small beeping sounds as the timer she set counts down. In one and a half minutes the doors will open for a few seconds to allow the shift change—and start the chain reaction that ends with us leaving this prison. Rory is standing near the cubicles holding four more backpacks of supplies to hand to the other players. He is also positioned there to signal to Juniper that the doors are opening.

Juniper's timer is at five seconds. I take a huge breath and slowly let it out. Everything that we've been working for for the past few months is all coming down to this. We cannot—we *will not*—screw it up now. I stand quietly as her watch counts down the last seconds: 3…2…1…

It's go time.

The timer hits zero, and suddenly everything is a blur. Rory comes bursting through the door and gives us a thumbs-up.

"Go, Juniper!" I yell. She nods and swipes across the screen of her device, enabling the command that releases the virus. We all sprint into the front room right as the second-shift people rush out of the doors.

"Come on, everyone! We don't have much time!" Crosby exclaims. The second shifters grab their packs from Rory. It's odd seeing them for more than a split second as we switch spots. It hits me—I barely know these people. They are just fellow players that I give an occasional smile or wave to. But there are more important things going on right now. Crosby is trying to summarize our escape plan for the second-shift crew; before now, they've only been able to hear bits and pieces when we traded shifts.

Less than thirty seconds after Juniper activates the virus, I hear the unmistakable sounds of it spreading. It's worse than nails on a chalkboard. The second-shift people—who have never experienced this—are panicking, and Crosby is unsuccessfully trying to calm them down.

"Now! The programmers are distracted, so they can't stop us! Everyone, hurry!" Juniper exclaims. We gather under the drop station and create a human pyramid in order to reach the trap door. Ada, the shortest of all of us, stretches to tape it open while carefully balancing on several people.

Although I am straining under the weight of the people I'm holding up, I manage to get a tiny glimpse of what is behind the door. It is pitch black—a seemingly endless tube with only the tiniest speck of light a hundred feet above to suggest there is an exit at all.

This part of the plan is simple. We each have two knives, and we are to stab the walls with our knives and pull ourselves up. *All* the way up. It's going to be like doing hundreds of pull-ups one after another. Maybe it won't be as terrible as it seems. We have all been training and building up our strength for years; a simple climb is going to be a breeze!

I hope.

We start helping people into the long tube one by one, with Ada taking the lead. Eventually, the human pyramid consists of only a few people, so we use furniture to hoist ourselves up. The ominous sounds of the virus aren't helping my nerves. After climbing on top of a sofa, table, and chair, I finally pull myself into the tube.

I pierce my knives into the cold wooden wall and hang on for dear life. The space is uncomfortably small, a narrow tube that would undoubtedly be terrifying to anyone with claustrophobia. Thankfully, that isn't too big of an issue for us. Over our years in the game, adapting to being in small spaces for long periods of time has proven to be a very necessary skill.

Once I've climbed just far enough to give Juniper some room, I shout for her to begin her trek. She stabs her knives into the wall and starts to work her way up. I continue to do the same, the slight grunts of exertion from my friends filling the air. I've already worked up a sweat, and we've barely started.

I'm getting a feeling that this is not going to be nearly as easy as I hoped.

After maybe a minute of climbing, everyone is completely inside the tube—even Juniper and her dangling legs. It's time to close the tube.

"Close it up, Juniper!" I remind her between breaths. She says thanks quietly and then, judging from the sounds of her fumbling with her pack, starts looking for her "special lock."

I have no idea how she made a virus-proof lock. How do you create a lock to barricade against something that's not even tangible? It sounds impossible—and to be honest, I thought it was. But somehow Juniper came up with a solution.

Once Juniper finds the lock, I reach out my hand, which she latches onto gratefully. She repositions herself so that she can place the lock without falling through. I'm a little surprised at the sight of the lock; it's not anything like what I expected. Instead of looking like a real padlock, it resembles a thin screen with an odd sticky coating covering it. There are a ton of buttons lining the side of it.

Juniper takes caution as she attaches the lock onto the bottom of the door. It's an awkward way to do it—what with her practically hanging upside down and all—but a few moments later and the job is done. Quiet cheers ring through the small space. We no longer have to rush to stay ahead of the virus! It's a huge weight off of our shoulders. My tense climbing immediately turns more relaxed. That's one less thing to worry about.

"You're awesome, Juniper!" Ada calls into the complete darkness.

"It's no big deal. I just…um…put some stuff tog—" Her sentence trails off into nothing.

The next few hours are grueling. Juniper and I are at the biggest disadvantage; we have only been training rigorously for the past year or two, while some of the others have decades of training under their belts. These past few weeks I've been trying to put in extra hours in the combat room for this exact reason, but it doesn't seem to be helping much at all. My arms are burning, and the literal light at the end of the tunnel doesn't seem to be getting any closer. No one talks much. It is mostly quiet grunts and an occasional complaint.

We take two water breaks and a meal break, but considering that we have to dangle from one arm or brace our feet against the sides of the tube to do so, they're not exactly restful.

There are a few close calls as we make our way up the tube, but thankfully, no serious accidents occur. The scariest one is when Ada's hand slips while she was taking a drink; thank goodness Rory catches her before she brought us all down with her.

It's one of the most terrifying experiences of my life. It's not just the close calls, though, it's everything. I never really thought that I would be climbing up a mile-long tube with two knives in a life-or-death situation. Let's just say I do not want to do it again.

What's almost worse than the pain is the boredom. It's complete silence except for grunts and people panting—not necessarily the nicest things to listen to when you're trying to ignore the pain creeping through your limbs. Lucky for us, Ada has our backs.

"Does anyone want to hear a story?" she asks, her sudden voice startling us. Ada is easily one of the strongest of us, so boredom is probably the only problem *she* is currently facing. After a moment of silence, there's a series of quiet agreements. I join in as well.

"I mean, I figured that since we are leaving this place, I might as well tell everyone my game origin story. Not a single person knows it, but I kind of feel like I should make it known. How I got in, right before we get out." Her strong voice echoes off the close walls.

Wow. I can't believe she hasn't told anyone her story! I'm her best friend, but even I've never heard it. Ada never really liked talking about her past with me, but I'd assumed that she'd already told it to some of the others. I didn't realize she hadn't told *anyone*. This should be interesting. I try to get a better grip on my knives as they threaten to slip out of my hands thanks to my sweaty palms.

"It started when I was a sophomore in high school. I don't know if you had guessed, but I was really athletic." I hear a faint scoff and an arrogant remark in Rory's unmistakable voice, followed by Ada threatening to bounce him off the wall. Even I can't hold in my laugh.

"Football was my thing! Little Ada was pumped for tryouts. I was going to be the best running back there. The tryouts came around, and unsurprisingly, I was the only girl. That stupid coach kicked me out in front of all those idiotic football players. They just couldn't stop laughing at the possibility of having a girl on the team. I admit, I felt pretty terrible."

"Oh, come on—we all know you would have kicked their butts if you had the chance!" I say, out of breath. I hear a few others chime in to agree, which makes Ada laugh.

"Please. Of course I would have. Anyway, even after I took it up with the principal, the coach

said no. I was furious. After a few weeks of training, I decided to go out for the hockey team. It
was an exact repeat of the football tryouts except
but more embarrassing. It might seem stupid
to me now, but I felt like it was the end of the
world."

"Teenagers!" Sawyer shouts jokingly. Everyone
laughs.

"Amen! I was fired up with anger and hurt
nonetheless. I mean, I knew my school was a little
sexist, but this was straight-up discrimination.
This is where it gets bad. I called up the principal
and asked him to put together an assembly so
that I could speak up against sexism. He obliged.
Everything seemed fine. Good, even! I mean, I
was using my experiences to help raise awareness
about issues, right?"

What's wrong with that? Her origin story
doesn't seem that bad.

"Wrong! My 'speech' was me basically screaming at the school and ranting in the most uncivil
way possible. I had a temper, okay? But if I were
to read that now—whew! I don't think even I
could resist laughing." An image of a younger
Ada aggressively yelling during an assembly pops
into my head, and I smile.

"But dang! I'd never been made fun of more in my entire life! I was the crazy feminist that no one liked. To be fair, I did kind of bring it upon myself, but they didn't have to be that brutal! So I had this whole overnight-personality-switch thing. I became a rude, rebellious brat." I snorted at her bluntness.

"What? It's true! Since everyone decided to hate me, I decided to hate everyone! It wasn't only at school—oh no! It was at home too! My poor mother." Ada adds jokingly. Rory whispers something to her that causes her to burst out laughing.

"I grew up in a pretty strict household. One of the rules was *no video games*. Obviously, thanks to my rebellious teenager phase, I went out and bought a video game console and tons of games. At first, I played just to make my mom mad, but then I actually began liking them. It was a way for me to work out my anger in a way that didn't result in total humiliation. I thought it was good for me for a while! Until I began to become reliant on them. Way too reliant. One thing led to another, and we all know what happened next!" It is quiet for a few seconds except for our labored breathing.

"Is it just me, or would everyone kill to see Ada as an angry teenager?" I comment with a laugh. Everyone heartily agrees and Ada chuckles. "At least we know you've had your temper all along" I add snarkily.

"Hey! I'm not that bad!"

"Sorry, sweetie, but you almost killed Ivy the first day. Remember the napkins?" Sawyer reminds us. I smile as the memory flashes across my mind. I remember how absolutely terrified I was! I did not expect her to become my closest friend in the game. I'm going to miss the good times with her.

At around the two-hour mark, the light at the top is much closer. It is only about forty feet away from me at this point. Our pace slowed after the first thirty minutes, but now everyone's energy is given a boost. We pick up the pace, working our already numb arms to the bone.

We are so close.

Up ahead, I see a small figure pulling herself over the edge and collapsing out of exhaustion. She lets out a happy *whoop* of excitement. Ada has made it!

More and more people reach the top: Luna, Rory, the people on second shift. When Crosby, who is right above me, makes it up, I put one last burst of energy into my climbing and propel myself over the edge.

Immediately, I collapse onto the cool stone floor, closing my eyes to protect them from the blinding light in the area that I have just entered. After more than two hours in complete darkness, it is going to take a while for my eyes to adjust to the well-lit room. I can't feel my limbs, I'm breathing hard, and I feel like fainting, but I've never felt better. We are one step closer to our freedom.

Once I have steadied myself enough to sit up, a short young woman from the second shift grasps my hand and pulls me to a standing position. I smile gratefully, and she returns it with a short but sweet nod. I brush off the dirt that has already started to accumulate on my pants and wait eagerly for Juniper to emerge from the darkness of the tube. About a minute passes, and I start to worry. Juniper should have been able to climb all the way up by now. I don't hear any grunts or other sounds, but then, Juniper is a quiet climber. *It's probably nothing*, I convince myself. I decide to get used to my surroundings in the meantime.

We're in a long, dingy hallway, with a low ceiling and stone walls. The floor is crawling with spiders, beetles, and many other bugs. The dark stone walls are damp with mold and mildew, and hair-like fractures trace the rock. Cobwebs line the ceiling's corners, and because the ceiling is quite low, it's easy to get the webs caught on our heads. (Jaclyn is *not* happy about that.) The hallway smells unpleasantly of moldy cheese. It's not my first choice of where to spend the next few hours, but it definitely trumps the tube!

Finally Juniper's head appears out of the darkness. She is dripping with sweat and her face is strained. I call Jaclyn over and we hoist Juniper up, despite our own sore arms. When we finally pull her out of the darkness, she lands in a heap of exhaustion on the floor. We give her a minute to collect herself and catch her breath.

"I'm sorry I took so long. I haven't had the best training," she admits with a grimace, gesturing to her barely-there arm muscles. We tell her not to worry about it, of course. In fact, it gave us more time to regroup.

"Phew, thanks!" Juniper says as she tries to catch her breath. I take a large gulp of water. It's a refreshing change for my parched throat. There is a bit of light chatter as we all start to prepare ourselves for the next part of our plan.

The first step of our escape is complete, but there is so much more to do before we are free.

CHAPTER 15

"Now, we need the map. Ivy, you have it, right?" Juniper asks, gesturing at my bag. I perk up and begin shuffling through the contents of my pack. Okay, not here. Maybe it's in here? Wait, what if I—never mind, got it! I pull out the fragile sheet and do my best to straighten the crumpled edges. I hand it to Juniper, who starts to lead us down the hallway. We have a long walk ahead of us. Not only will my arms be so sore that I can barely move them, but my legs will be too. Yay.

To distract myself from the boredom and the continuous ache in my arms, I make up a small challenge for myself. My goal is to try to meet all the "new" people—all of the second-shift people other than Jaclyn—before we escape.

Jaclyn is the only person on second shift that I've gotten to know. She was a big help to me when I first got to the game, and I really do like her company. Our talks have been short, usually in ten minute increments before my shift begins—and through a wall. Despite the odd circumstances, I've enjoyed getting to know her.

I would have loved to talk to the others before now, but they've always seemed busy talking to one another, deep in thought, or just plain not in the mood. After the first month or so, I fell into a routine and never really tried reaching out to them. I told myself I eventually would, but I never got around to it. This is my last chance.

I start with the shy girl who helped me up out of the tube earlier. She has short, fiery-red hair, fair skin, and freckles dotting her nose. Her eyes are a light green; they complement her hair perfectly. I recognize her immediately. Corrine was my ride-or-die character for the months that I was hooked on the game.

Oh my gosh—I must have played her half to death!

I feel guilt rising inside me, but I shove it away. That was years ago! And I can't just ignore her. I need to fix this before I go. I may never see her again, but at least I'll know that I made this right.

I catch up with the kind-looking girl and introduce myself. She turns in surprise.

"Oh! Hello there! I'm, well, Corrine," she replies, tucking a strand of hair behind her ear shyly.

"You sure about that?" I tease. We both laugh. "Hey, before we talk, I'd just like to say that I'm really sorry." Corrine gives me a confused glance, and I signal for her to wait for me to explain. "Look, when I was still obsessed with the game, you were my favorite player. I don't even remember how many times I made you go on runs for hours on end. I feel terrible; I can't imagine how horrible that was for you." Corrine pauses before giving me a wide smile.

"Aww, you don't have to be sorry! That was a long time ago, and it helped build my endurance! But I'm flattered that I was your favorite player." We both laugh, and thankfully, the twinge of guilt starts to fade. Her forgiveness doesn't make it disappear right away, but I know that with time my guilt will be gone. I'm glad that I apologized to her.

For the next hour, I talk with Corrine. She has been here for three years, and was always the shy, odd one out in her shift. Corrine is only a little bit older than me and *also* has an annoying little brother. (His name is Max.) She and I are so much alike. But even more than myself, she reminds me of my mother; they have the same gray-green eyes. There is so much more to Corrine than I would have thought without talking to her!

During my chat with Corrine, our group travels about a third of the way towards our destination—or, at least, where we think our destination is supposed to be. Despite the fact that we have walked almost six miles, we're still in a narrow stone hallway. There have been only a few turns and no change of scenery at all. It's getting a little old, but I'll take this over climbing any day.

Corrine says she is best friends with Jaclyn, but she doesn't talk much with anyone else in the game. At first I'm a little surprised that she and Jaclyn get along so well. But, when I think about it, I realize their personalities complement each other perfectly.

Jacyln is just the type of loyal friend that Corrine needs to stand up for her and stick by her throughout the game. From what I've learned from Corrine, she's too sweet to do stuff like that by herself; Jaclyn probably always takes care of those things. Corrine, on the other hand, is just the person to help Jaclyn calm down when she is freaking out. I can tell that Corrine has always and will always be there for Jaclyn. Their bond is obviously really tight; it makes me happy that they each have someone to lean on!

Also, Corrine can crack some pretty good jokes.

As much as I hate to leave her, I want to meet *everyone*, so I say a temporary goodbye and casually stride up to the next "new" person I see. This time, I don't have to initiate the conversation.

"Well, hello there! You're Ivy, am I correct? Tony Smith," the boy says brightly, extending his hand for a sideways handshake while we continue walking. I grin and nod happily.

It isn't hard to get to know Tony. He has a quirky personality and he loves to talk—about anything. He has very strong opinions about any controversial topic, and from what I can tell, he voices them to anyone who will listen. During our trek, he also rambles on about the paranormal, conspiracy theories, urban legends, and other creepy stuff. The dingy hallway setting helps set the mood, and I can't say I'm not a bit freaked out. I mean, what about the idea of killer porcelain dolls coming to life *isn't* scary?

Tony is about six years older than me, and got transported into the game at the same age that I did. He has long black hair and cryptic, dark-brown eyes. My conversation with Tony is worlds different than the one I had with Corrine. I can see why they haven't really thought to talk; their personalities are polar opposites. But they are each so likeable in their own way.

"Why were you talking to Corrine over there?" Tony asks out of the blue. Maybe it's my imagination, but his tone seems to have soured.

"What do you mean?" He gives me a look of surprise.

"Are you serious? She's so rude!" he blurts out. I almost stop walking.

"What? No, she isn't!" I say with a nervous laugh. I'm obviously missing something here.

He scoffs. "Please. She always acts like she thinks she's better than you." I'm shocked. We can't be talking about the same Corrine.

"Um…I think she's just shy," I say quietly. Immediately I can tell that was the wrong thing to say. Tony looks ready to get into a full-fledged argument. "Uh—never mind! What were you saying about that one story about the dolls?" I ask with forced enthusiasm. His hard expression softens, and we fall back into our conversation.

I don't know why I thought that everyone would be friends in the game. I argue with Crosby a lot, but it's never with actual malice. Sure, he and Ada don't get along very well, but they're always civil. Tony looked like he was about to explode when he mentioned Corrine's name, and he's the most easy-going person I've met in the game! I can't see why Corinne would have annoyed him, and my confusion won't stop nagging at me. I try to convince myself that maybe they just didn't get along, but I can't help think that there's more to it than that.

We have walked miles at this point. Luckily, my talk with Tony is lively enough to distract me from the growing pain in my legs. I am so caught up with our conversation that I don't notice the rest of the group has come to a sudden stop. I smash into Ada and almost cause a domino effect on everyone in front of me.

"Ivy!" Crosby hisses. I wince. I peek over Ada's shoulder and see that we have come to a dead end. Oops. I guess we're turning back now. Juniper must have misinterpreted the map. That's odd; Juniper does everything right.

I shrug it off and turn around. Tony places a firm hand on my shoulder, stopping me in my tracks. I give him a confused look; he replies by simply gesturing to what is happening in front of us.

Juniper is studying the map; a few others are crowded around her to help identify the problem. Suddenly, she hands the map to Ada and begins to inspect the walls of the hallway, running her hands against its sides, grasping and pulling at any ridges. Jaclyn catches on quickly and starts searching the floor. Rory, who's the tallest, easily begins looking on the ceiling. Although I'm clueless as to what we're looking for (and feeling insecure about it) I mimic the others' actions in one of the unsearched areas.

After almost twenty minutes of searching, during which I still have no clue what we are doing, I find and pull on a random ridge. It slides towards me smoothly. That's weird—this rock feels just like a lever. Wait a second—Juniper said that The GameMaster would try to throw us off with obstacles. We're looking for a secret passageway.

CHAPTER 16

"Um…guys?" I call. Heads turn. The others clearly aren't expecting anything important, so they're pleasantly surprised to see me pointing to the lever I've discovered. A few cheers sound, and as if on cue, a large wall gives way to an opening. I peek inside hopefully only to see another long hallway, identical to this one. Ugh. More walking. Lucky for me, Luna calls a water-and-snack break, and we all sit down. I sigh in relief. It has never felt so good to sit on the floor. The sound of bags opening echoes through the hallway as we all grab our forms of sustenance.

I gulp down a couple sips of water, forcing myself not to drink the whole bottle; we still have quite a way to go. For a snack, I pull out a bag of dried vegetables from a past dinner. They're a little crushed from the weight of the rest of the items in my bag, but I'm so hungry that I don't mind.

I wolf down the veggies and clean myself up with a small napkin. Jaclyn and I discuss how the real world is going to look to us now while we wait for the others, but it's mostly quiet. We burned through a lot of energy today, and we have so much longer to go. Wasting our energy on conversation isn't exactly our first priority. (I guess my whole meeting-people game is a bit counter-productive, but that's for distraction!) Not much later, we start down the next endless stone hallway.

My mind shifts back to my "game," and I march up to my last, and seemingly least friendly, new person.

"Hello, I'm Ivy!" I say brightly. Silence. Only about thirty seconds later does he reply with a peep, so tiny that I almost don't even catch it.

"Ron."

Judging from the volume of his voice and the length of time it took him to reply, there's no way I am going to get this dude to say much of anything. So I tell him my life story— blabbering on and probably annoying the poor man to death. Halfway through one story, he cracks a miniature smile, which I consider a win.

After a little while, I eventually run out of things to monologue about, so I end up just saying what's on my mind.

"I wonder what happened between Tony and Corinne," I say thoughtfully. Out of the corner of my eye, I see Ron's eyes widen a little and he tenses up. His reaction is odd, but nothing too out of the ordinary. It's not like he actually knows…unless— Nah.

Then again, quiet people always know more than you'd expect.

"You definitely know!" I exclaim as Ron tries to cover up his reaction. He shakes his head unconvincingly.

"Oh, would you just spill it? I've been wanting to know this all day," I plead. Ron gives me an unsure look and hesitates as I beg one last time.

"Fine," he grumbles. I clap my hands together in excitement, and he rolls his eyes.

"If you tell anybody…," he warns. I make a show of dramatically zipping up my mouth and throwing away the key, earning myself another unimpressed look from Ron. Sheesh, tough crowd.

"Tony had a big crush on Jaclyn, but she never really paid any attention to him. They were maybe acquaintances. Then, Corrine arrived in the game and she and Jaclyn became best friends within days. He was really frustrated." I raise my eyebrows in surprise. First of all, this is the longest Ron had ever spoken, and secondly, I had no idea. I don't really know what I thought their feud was built on, but it definitely wasn't this.

"Then, when he tried to talk to Corinne, she wouldn't talk to him. Too shy, I think, but Tony thought that she was mocking him for not being able to get Jaclyn to talk to him. And once he had a vendetta against her, she started disliking him." I grimace. That must be hard on both of them: Corinne having someone hate her and not even knowing why, and Tony thinking that she was mocking him in the first place.

"That's terrible. But you know the whole story, so why don't you tell them? It could solve the problem," I propose. Ron scoffs.

"No one's going to listen to me."

I wag my finger at him. "You don't know unless you try!" I'm met with quiet once again and a small shrug. I guess his little talking streak is over.

We stop for our last snack break. Ron and I sit by each other in silence, munching. I take a big swig of water, leaving only a couple drops at the bottom of the bottle. Thank goodness we only have about an hour to go- hopefully. Walking through a cramped hallway for over five hours with ten other people who are all sweaty and worn out is *not* fun. Especially when half of you don't even know each other very well. Nonetheless, we trudge on.

Juniper has been increasingly on edge throughout the journey. Now her nervousness is definitely peaking.

"Juniper?" She jumps but relaxes when she sees it's only me.

"I'm fine," she insists. She turns her back and walks away from me. Great, the silent treatment. I ignore it and go back to talking with some of the people I've met today. I'm not letting her weird attitude ruin what could be my last few minutes with my friends!

CHAPTER 17

ONE HOUR LATER

We are seconds away from the portal—I can see it! Everyone is beaming…except Juniper, who looks as if she is about to burst into tears. It's the oddest thing, but I brush off her strange expression. We made it! All of our effort is finally paying off! I break into a run with everyone following close behind me. For the first time all day, I don't even mind the aching pain in my legs. Actually, that's the last thing on my mind at the moment.

Each step towards the portal feels like a weight being lifted off of my shoulders. It's one less second I have to spend trapped here.

We all pause in front of the portal to our freedom, taking in the sheer enormity of the moment. Here we are, staring at what looks like a scrap of galaxy embedded in a black frame. This small portal represents everything we have been looking forward to for years—for some, decades.

Everyone stands there and stares. I would have thought we'd leap into the portal the instant it came into view, but the reality is more complicated than that. We aren't just saying goodbye to the game; we're saying goodbye to each other. We'll still talk in the real world, but it won't be the same. We'll be thousands of miles away from each other, living our own lives.

This is the moment I've been dreading. I can't bear to say goodbye to my best friends. I've spent years with these people. They know the real Ivy— the Ivy I've grown into since I arrived. They've been there with me through thick and thin. They *are* my family. I know I'm going to burst into tears if I try to talk, so we all exchange quiet hugs. Each one means something different. Some hugs mean "thanks." Others, "I'll miss you." And a few, "I don't want to leave you."

Sawyer pulls me into an embrace. We just stand there, squeezing each other tightly. My favorite game-buddy. One of the first people to befriend me in the game. And now I have to leave him.

He steps back and gives me a smile as his eyes well up with tears. I return both smile and unshed tears. Luna comes up to me next. Her gentle embrace almost causes my tears to spill over. Even though I didn't spend a lot of time with Luna, I knew I could count on her to talk to. No matter when, or what I was going through, she was always there for me. I put my hand on her shoulder and look her in the eyes for one last smile. Oh, how I'm going to miss them all!

Crosby tries to say goodbye as quickly as possible, but I stop him and make sure to give him a long, drawn-out hug. From his uncomfortable squirming, I can tell that he's not used to this touchy-feely stuff, but it makes me smile. We've had our differences, but Crosby has kept us safe for all this time, and I can't thank him enough for that.

I walk up to Rory and give him a quick bear hug. He pulls away and steps on my shoe playfully as his form of goodbye. I smile sadly. He's been like a brother to me; I don't think he's ever failed to make me laugh. I'm going to miss seeing his stupid face every morning.

When Ada walks up to me, I have to calm myself down before she even tries to hug me. This is my best friend we're talking about here— my stubborn, bad-advice-giving, soon-to-be-an-awesome-mom best friend. Our hug is the quickest, but it holds the most meaning in my heart. I remember our first day together—Ada told me that there was no way to escape. Look where we are now. Who would have thought we'd make it this far?

Juniper avoids every goodbye anyone tries to share with her, and instead sits sulkily in front of the portal. I don't know what is up with her, but that doesn't stop me from giving her a tight goodbye squeeze. No matter what she is feeling now, Juniper is one of my best friends. After everything we have gone through together, I think we should at least say a small goodbye.

Once everyone (well, *almost* everyone) has said goodbye to everyone else, and most sad tears have turned into happy grins, we gather in one final huddle.

"Listen up, everyone. Some of us have known each other for longer than we've known our biological families, and some of us just met hours ago, but no matter what happens, we'll always be there for each other in the real world. We've bonded over something that we would rather forget, but it will stay with us forever. We might as well look on the bright side—now we all have friends for life." Cheers sound at the end of Crosby's short but heartfelt speech, which brings even more tears to my eyes.

We assemble into a rough line, everyone playfully shoving me to the front. I glance back at the faces of each of my friends, a sad smile on my lips.

I can't believe we made it. This is the moment I've dreamed of for two years. The moment where we finally win. I get to leave all of this behind and start fresh; I am getting a second chance at my life! I step up to the portal, but I'm shaking. All I can see is the purple-blue swirl in front of me that leads to my fresh start.

Memories of life in the game flash before my eyes: my first day as a character, meeting Juniper, our hilarious attempts at group activities, prepping for the escape. Everything in those two years played such a big part in shaping my personality, and now it's time to let it all go. This is it.

This is goodbye.

Goodbye, work shifts. Goodbye, control room. Goodbye, incredible food. Goodbye, couch in the living room. Goodbye, my *bed.* Goodbye, my friends. Goodbye, *Escape the War.* A single tear slips from my eye as I place my foot into the portal—the portal to my new-old life.

Someone stops me before I can step in.

"Juniper! What are you doing?" I ask. Her hands grasp my wrists fiercely, but she won't meet my eyes. The line disperses immediately and everyone gathers around us. Juniper is crying. *Really* crying. Sobbing-her-eyes-out crying.

"I'm sorry, Ivy." That's all she says before it happens.

Juniper takes another handheld device from her pocket, and I give her a confused look. Where did she get that? And why does she even need it? She avoids my gaze. After a second of hesitation, she finally presses a button on the device. I feel an odd tugging sensation on my limbs, and every second it begins to grow stronger.

"Juniper…Juniper!" I say, becoming more alarmed by the second. I try to fight the pull, but I am unsuccessful. I hear confused cries from the others as they experience the same sensation. The portal slips further away with each moment.

Eventually, this unseen force drags each of us far enough so that we are trapped against the wall. Again, I struggle against the invisible wires restraining me, but I can't manage to free myself.

Juniper cringes back, not looking at any of us. Why isn't she trapped, too? Nothing makes sense.

"What are you *doing*, Juniper?" I exclaim. We were just about to escape!

Attempting to contain her sobs, Juniper takes a deep, shaky breath. Her words are quiet and hesitant, but that doesn't stop pain from lancing through me when she says them.

"I…I made a deal with the GameMaster."

CHAPTER 18

The GameMaster. The person who trapped us in this prison for years on end. The person who ruined the lives of countless other people just so her game would top the charts. The person who *destroyed* us.

My head hurts with the stress of forcing denial through it. No. Juniper would never do that.

After calming her ragged breathing, Juniper reluctantly continues. "I made a deal with the GameMaster," she repeats, louder this time. The others, who hadn't heard her the first time, gasp.

"You're kidding, right? This is some sort of cruel joke?" I spit out through fake laughs. Juniper looks at me with pure sadness in her eyes, and my smile fades in a second. Beside me, I see Ada's face reddening with anger.

"Oh Ivy, I wish I were kidding," she whispers, fighting back tears. I don't respond. I don't think I can do this. I can't go through *another* betrayal.

"Please let me explain. Please, Ivy," Juniper begs pathetically. I cringe at the sound of my name in her voice. We stand in silence for a moment due to my refusal to answer. She continues anyway.

"I know you hate me. But please. Just listen to me. None of this would have even happened if the game hadn't been doing so poorly," she adds bitterly. I glance up, breaking my frozen stance. Juniper spots my sudden change, and she begins to elaborate.

"The popularity of *Escape the War* has been decreasing the past few years; people just don't play it as much anymore. That wouldn't have mattered, but the GameMaster refuses to have her game beaten by anyone else's." That doesn't make sense; what about the "orientation" video we all saw when we first came here? It said that *Escape the War* had been the most popular game for over twenty-five years!

"The intro video was all lies. It—she didn't want anyone to think of her as a failure," Juniper says, answering my unspoken question. I scoff. This is about the GameMaster's ego—*again*? I ball up my fists.

"The GameMaster told me she was going to program a completely new game with new real-life characters, a new plot...one that is more addictive than ever. It would top the charts for decades, surpassing *Escape the War*. But first, she needed to get rid of this game totally," she continues. I pause. If she has to delete the game, does that mean we are free to go back to our old lives? I let my anger go, and a shrivel of hope inside me begins to blossom. But if we're going home, why does Juniper look so miserable?

"My addiction happened like everyone else's. But one thing was different. When I was chosen to transfer to the game, I didn't fall through the drop chute first; I fell into the GameMaster's lair." We shoot each other confused looks.

"She brought me there because of a deal we made a few years ago. When I was picked for the game, she realized that, with my coding experience, I could figure out how to escape and destroy everything. So she told me I could leave the game, go back to my normal life, but I would have to help her destroy the game first. And only if I was the only one to escape. The rest of you would have to...to...die." The little hope I had is crushed into a million pieces and my anger comes flooding back. So is Juniper telling us that together, she and The GameMaster are going to delete *Escape the War*—and take us with it?

"But why?" Luna whimpers, the first peep she has made all this time. I see Juniper lock eyes with Luna's sorrow-filled ones and then tears away her gaze.

"*Escape the War* is going to fail, and she doesn't want anything as a reminder that she didn't succeed. But if something were to mysteriously delete the whole game before it flopped, then people would only feel bad for her. It would save her reputation. As for the…other aspect…one person escaping takes so much energy that it almost causes the whole system to shut down. All eleven of us? The entire building would probably explode," she replies hesitantly. And, so what? That's worth our *lives*?

"When I first got the threats a few years ago, I didn't want to do it. I couldn't bring myself to hurt y—anyone. But you don't understand what she said to me, what she did to me. I had been getting messages from random numbers for months, telling me how painful my death would be if I didn't agree. Or how everyone in my life would forget about me. Her threats were so scary, so *real*. Please, you all have to understand!"

I shake my head. No. I *don't* "have to understand."

"I walked around every day for weeks in a state of terror. I couldn't breathe without being terrified that she was going to spring something on me! I had no choice!" At this point, I can't tell who she is trying to convince, us or herself.

"The day I landed in *Escape the War*, she forced me to swear on my life that I would help her—and now that I was in the game, she literally had my life in her hands. I couldn't break the deal even if I wanted to. I'm so, so sorry." I shoot her a disgusted look in response to her feeble apology. I'm such an idiot. I was the one who convinced the gang to trust Juniper and let her make the virus. I was the one who got Crosby to forgive her after the virus slip-up. And now it's my fault that we are all going to die.

"That's why when I first arrived, my guard was up. I hated that I had to do this. I didn't want to get too close to anyone because—"

"Because you knew in the end you would betray us," Sawyer says. His joking nature is gone, replaced with stone-cold resentment.

"'Accidentally' releasing the virus wasn't really an accident, was it?" Ada starts angrily, struggling to release herself from the invisible force and get to Juniper. She realizes that she is unable to break free and gestures for Juniper to come toward her. Juniper nervously complies. Bad call—you don't mess with Ada.

Ada grabs Juniper by the shirt and yanks her forward. The fact that they are only inches apart helps make Ada's point. Unsurprisingly, Juniper is trembling.

"You were *trying* to kill us? I can't believe I ever trusted you! I can't believe—" Ada's voice has risen to a yell. Juniper shuffles backwards and meekly interrupts her.

"No! I- I'm sorry! I was supposed to release it then, and I did—but I couldn't *kill* you. I'm not a murderer! Everyone had been so kind to me. We were friends. I couldn't bring myself to do it; I *had* to give you at least a chance." Ada lets out an icy laugh.

I scoff again. How touching. She doesn't seem to have any trouble killing us now! Obviously, her loyalty lies with the "GameMaster"—not with the people who took her in and treated her with love.

"It wasn't an accident. But I care about you. I really do. I know I seem like a horrible person right now, but you have to understand that I'm just trying to survive! I risked my life to save you then! I—"

"Shut up," Rory snarls. Juniper does, and silence envelops the room.

"The virus will be here soon. I never fully closed the door. Only the part that transfers humans. The virus can—it *will*—still come through." The room is silent once again. I can feel Crosby's furious scowl boring into the back of my head, but I can't think about that.

I can't think about anything. Juniper, one of my best friends. Someone I took in, made memories with. Someone I thought of as family. She betrayed me. She betrayed *all* of us.

My fury is dissolving into a painfully familiar feeling. This is too similar to what happened to me before *Escape the War*. Back when the real world was my reality.

Back when Jane betrayed me.

Everything's coming together so fast: why I felt like I *knew* Juniper the first time we met. The way we got along so quickly. Why Juniper always looks at me guiltily. Why she was *reciting our handshake* when I walked in on her working. My mind is whizzing as the pieces of the puzzle all fall into place. It's been right in front of me this whole time; I just never wanted to see it. I couldn't bring myself to accept the truth.

The GameMaster may have given Jane a new appearance and a new name, but I would always recognize my best friend.

"*Coward!*" Ada screeches. I look into Juniper's hazel eyes and finally let go. My tears are coming fast now.

Not Juniper. *Jane.* That is the Jane I played dress-up with in preschool, whose house I knew better than my own, who promised she would never leave me. But it's also the Jane who became popular, ignored me for months, and made fun of me time and time again. I don't know which Jane is real.

"J- J...Jane?" I whisper. I want so badly to believe that my best friend wouldn't betray me again. She tenses up and shoots me a sorrowful glance. Her dim eyes fill with tears that spill over. It is true. I clamp my hand over my mouth to stop myself from crying out.

"The virus will be here soon," she repeats, this time in a regretful whisper. She's avoiding our eyes again. Jane nervously glances to her left and right, then walks toward the portal. Before she steps in, she looks back at me, as if trying to make a decision.

She shoves the device into my hand.

"This button will release everyone from the wall, but it will also close the portal and open up a maze. The portal will reopen somewhere in the maze, but the virus is spreading. You *have* to find the portal. It's the only way you will survive. I'm sorry."

I stare at Jane's disguise, her tearstained olive skin, choppy black hair, and embarrassed frown. My imagination flashes, replacing Jane's mask with her real chestnut-brown hair, pale skin, and unmistakable smile. The image disappears as quickly as it came, and I'm faced again with a teary-eyed "Juniper."

"Please. I have to explain, Ivy—I can't live knowing that you don't understand." I scoff for what seems like the thousandth time today. She seems to have been living fine with the fact that she ruined my life until now! Despite my attitude clearly encouraging her to give it up, she does the exact opposite and attempts to explain.

"That first day of freshman year, that's when the GameMaster told me that I would have to betray you to survive. That in a matter of years I would have to leave you to die if I wanted to live... so...I cut you off. But no matter how hard I tried, I never stopped caring about you, Ivy. I can't even begin to describe how sorry I am. Even though I know you can never forgive me for what I've done, just know that you will *always* be my best friend" Her voice breaks slightly, and she scrambles to take a deep breath. Memories flash through my head of our friendship snapping in half.

Sorry? Does she really think one "sorry" is going to undo all of her selfish choices, or fix the hole in my heart? I am fuming. Everyone around me attempts to inch away.

"Well, if you really were sorry, you wouldn't have saved *yourself*! If you were sorry, you would have rather died than betrayed us. If you were sorry, I wouldn't be *standing right here*!" My voice quavers with a mixture of passion and rage. Jane trembles, and even though I am only an inch taller than she is, I feel as if I am towering over a mouse.

Jane goes in for a hug, but instead of an embrace, all my pain and all my fury are released in a sharp slap across her face. She staggers backwards, grasping her cheek. I feel guilt begin to rise, but I shove it away. A slap is the least I can do.

Jane lowers her eyes and takes her hand from her cheek, revealing a splotchy red spot. She slowly turns around and walks to the portal. Each step seems to be taunting us. That should have been us. We deserve to escape, not her.

"I never meant to hurt you," she croaks quietly. Jane sounds so broken that I feel sorry for her for a second. Only a second, though. I stay silent.

With one last look at me, she steps into the portal. In seconds, she's disappeared. I clench my hand around the device, resisting the urge to smash it against the wall. Maybe that would help these feelings go away.

"Press the button," Sawyer spits out furiously. I click it and we're all released from our invisible restraints. The portal vanishes immediately. All of the walls open up, revealing hundreds of long, winding hallways. It's overwhelming.

Crosby snaps into leadership mode, trying to downplay the shocking chain of events that have just occurred. It's what he does—he leads us, even in times of peril. "Listen, I know the past ten minutes have been...interesting, but our only hope to stay alive is in those hallways. If Juniper—Jane—ugh! If *she* is telling the truth, we do have a chance of survival. Groups of two! Split up, a group per hallway! Check every corner. Yell if you find it." He pauses, as if debating whether to say something else.

"Also, say goodbye, our chances aren't good," Crosby finishes ruefully. I wipe away my tears, and we all crowd in for one last group hug. The painfully sentimental gesture is interrupted by a loud robotic snarl. It pierces through the hallways, the deadliness of whatever it is apparent in its ear-splitting volume. What in the world is that? Someone gasps loudly.

"No. No, no, no!" Jaclyn whimpers, abandoning her usually composed nature.

"What's wrong?" Corrine asks, her arms steadying Jaclyn's terrified tremors. Tony rolls his eyes and scoffs.

"Please! Stop acting like you actually care about her," Tony snarls. Corrine whips her head around and glares at him.

"Could you stop talking for one second? No one cares what you think!" she yells, pulling Jaclyn closer. Tony opens his mouth to retort back, but I stop them.

"Stop it! Now is not the time!" I say sternly, meeting their eyes. They back down and Corrine resumes comforting Jaclyn. Tony sulks in the corner. Jaclyn manages to pull herself together.

"I…I'm the only one of us who's ever made it to the boss of the game." My mouth falls open.

The actual boss. I've only heard legends from Luna about people making it to the boss. There are so many obstacles it's barely possible to get through the first few parts of the game, let alone all the way to the end. I never imagined that one of us had actually made it to the final boss.

"That's the sound the boss makes. The boss. It's coming," she cries, burying herself in Corinne's comforting embrace. I've never seen Jaclyn like this, but we can't focus on her panic now. Now not only do we have to worry about the virus, the practically unbeatable boss is after us too.

"Of course." Ron slaps his palm to his forehead. "The GameMaster probably suspected Juniper would try to help us. She must have programmed the boss to come after us as a precaution," he mutters.

"How do we stop it?" Ada asks desperately.

"We can't. We have to fight," Sawyer answers.

CHAPTER 19

Another roar comes from around the corner. The floor shakes as the boss approaches.

I take my weapons from my bag and slide my knives into my belt. My pistol stays in my hands.

"Don't look back. No second guessing," Rory yells as the noises get louder.

Ada unsheathes her sword and brandishes it in front of her. Her eyes are full of fire, but the expression plastered on her face as she prepares to fight for her life is deadly cold.

"Communicate. If we listen to each other we can get through this," Rory continues. He has to raise his voice to be heard over the increasingly loud noise of the beast we are about to encounter.

I slowly bring the gun up and point it at the opening the boss is about to come through. I'm shaking so much that I can't hold it straight. The gun quavers violently, straying further and further from my target. The more I feel my nerves, the worse my aim becomes, and we haven't even begun fighting yet. I can't fight right now—I'm going to get us killed!

A hand rests on my shoulder. "You can do this." Ada's reassuring voice stops my tremors and I take a deep breath. She is right; I can't quit now. My revelation happens just in time. A huge monster emerges from the hallway, and for a second, I am frozen in my footsteps.

The bottom half of the boss is a tank. Its two chained tracks screech mercilessly as it moves towards us. Not one, not two, but *three* enormous turrets are mounted on the outside of the tank. The top half is roughly humanoid in shape and built of sharp strips of scrap metal. It's similar to the guards protecting the boss I encountered thousands of times on my runs—but much worse. Long, curved swords dripping blood take the place of fingers. The lights that serve as its eyes burn a sickly green, and the mouth is a giant revolving saw, buzzing with electricity.

"We fight together; we die together!" Rory screams, his battle cry launching us into action. It's now or never.

Rory takes the first shot, cracking the monster's left eye. The green light goes out.

I whip out my knives. I aim first for the revolving tracks of the tank in hopes of restraining the monster's movement. Corinne spots my idea and sprints towards me, ducking to avoid the trail of bullets blasting from a turret.

Corrine is also armed with throwing knives; with both of us, there may be hope. We throw knife after knife, managing to lodge a few in each track. Corrine may have been a little shy when I first met her, but she is going hard at the boss. Almost every knife she throws pierces the conveyor belt in a perfect spot. But we are going to need a lot more than one or two perfect shots to stop this enormous, relentless thing.

She keeps whispering "For Jaclyn!" every time she throws her knives. It makes sense— Corrine is Jaclyn's best friend. Of course she knew about Jaclyn's encounter with the boss before anyone else did. No wonder she's firing all of her anger at this beast; it has pained her friend so much.

We are starting to run out of knives, but Corrine's determined nature doesn't falter. Every time we miss and a track just rolls over our knives, she shouts encouragement at me and we go at it harder.

Sixteen knives: that's all we have. And it takes all sixteen of them to finally stop it. The engine roars, struggling to push through the many knives blocking its movement, but there's no use.

"Yes!" I exclaim, high-fiving Corrine's bruised and raw hand with my identical one. Her soot-smeared face bears a look of pride. She doesn't need to tell me why. I can already see Jaclyn smiling at her from the other side of the monster.

The boss roars in frustration at its inability to move, then fires a missile right at us. I grab Corrine's arm and dive out of the way, mere moments from having our heads taken off.

From the corner of my eye I see Ada hacking away at the turrets with her sword. She has almost totally severed one from the tank when a long-bladed hand reaches for her. I scream as Rory leaps up and grabs the metal arm. With a yell, he uses his considerable strength to snap the arm almost in half. Taking advantage of the opportunity, Ada severs the arm completely and hurls it away from them. Rory staggers back from the beast, his hands torn and bloody after hanging onto its sharp metal. Seeing his feeble state, Corrine rushes over to him, tears a strip of fabric off her shirt, and bandages his hand with it. I yell at her to grab a miracle pill from her bag, and she nods, immediately stuffing one into Rory's hand. We need everyone to be in tip-top shape at all times during this fight; we can't afford to have Rory partially injured.

The little damage we've been able to inflict on the boss doesn't seem to have much effect, though. The only things in our favor are its inability to move and one missing turret. But even that much progress is about to be lost—the boss is clearly about to break through the knives in its tracks. There's no time to make a break for it.

Ron and Sawyer are teamed up in the corner, trying to come up with a plan. Sawyer's brows are furrowed in intense thought, and Ron's eyes are closed as he mumbles scientific gibberish that I don't understand. I hate it. I hate it because it reminds me of *her*. Look at my pathetic state—even in the midst of a deadly battle, I'm reminded of Jane.

I can make out a few snippets of their conversation, but I'm immediately occupied with my own problems. The boss has broken out of the knife-restricted movement and is aiming its remaining bladed hand at me.

I dive out of the way and sprint around the claws of death. I consider taking a risk and going into one of the hallways, but I know that the boss will just come after me.

I try to speed up, but I'm already at a full sprint, and the boss is gaining on me every second. I am inches away from total mutilation.

"Help!" I cry as my legs threaten to give way. Jaclyn charges at the hand and proceeds to weave her spear through the blades before twisting it and pulling down sharply. The blades snap off the monster. I stop running and give her a quick, grateful smile for saving my life, but other than that, there isn't much to smile about.

Mere seconds later, blades slide out from the arms of the boss, regenerating on *both* sides. It's like we haven't done any damage at all.

"What?!" I shriek, hacking at the newly re-grown hand with one of the previous hand's swords.

"We can't win!" Jaclyn screams over the snarls of the monster.

I grimace worriedly in response as I pull out my gun and send a few bullets through the blades. There's no time to worry about winning; we are barely even *surviving* at this point. Using the end of her spear, Jaclyn manages to block several attacks. Like Corrine, she fights like a warrior.

Her model-esque body attacks the moves fiercely but elegantly. Her hair whips around as we fight, the wave of blonde threatening to smack me in the face.

Despite the fact that we are in the midst of an intense battle, I can't help but be reminded of the first time I saw Jaclyn in a movie. She was in a fight scene, and even though at the time she was acting, she looked just as fierce as she did now. I think that's when ten-year-old Ivy became obsessed with her.

Jaclyn puts her heart into everything she does. I saw it in the way she acted and modeled before the game, and I've seen it in her runs every day since I arrived. Now I see it in the way she fights. Jaclyn makes it a point to dedicate herself to everything, and I think that's why I'm drawn to her—and why we are such good friends.

My thoughts are interrupted by a quick jab from the bladed hand. One sword slices my arm, leaving a shallow gash. I gasp, but keep fighting. This is nothing compared to what I've experienced in the game. My arm burns and blood drips from the wound, but I refuse to give up.

"Yes, we can win, Jaclyn!" Sawyer shouts from the corner. My ears perk up even as the pain in my arm intensifies. There's hope? Luna and Crosby's loud fighting grunts from across the room fill the air. They are battling the boss's saw-mouthed head.

"Are you going to tell us the plan or not?" Crosby yells to Sawyer and Ron, winded.

"The virus will be here in seconds! We need to stop the boss from moving and keep it right here. The virus will destroy the boss completely, but we have to run. If we are going to survive, we need to go *now!*" Sawyer screams. I can already see the back of the room disintegrating into black ashes.

Ada hurls herself at the monster, sticking her enormous sword straight into the left conveyor belt. Rory comes charging from the right, mirroring Ada's technique. The monster screeches and aims bullets at each of us. We dodge them, although one grazes Crosby's shoulder. He yelps in pain but brushes it off and continues fighting.

It's amazing—by expanding on the tactic Corrine and I used, they manage to stop the boss, hopefully long enough for us to escape. We can't fight any longer; we have to run.

I grab Jaclyn's arm. We drop all of our weapons and run, ducking as we swerve around the boss's hand.

"Duck, Ivy!" Ron screams—the loudest I've ever heard him—as we run for the exit into a hallway. Several bullets shriek by me, just above my head. I'm getting light-headed. Somehow in the midst of our frantic escape, I end up next to Ada. Jaclyn's hand slips from my grasp, and she is lost in the crowd. I hear a few terrified yells and someone gasps in pain.

My legs are pumping faster than they ever have before. My senses feel alive with terror. I've never been more scared in my life, but the maze is so close. We don't even know if the boss is still stuck in place; no one dares to look back.

In the last few seconds before we slip into the hallway, I hear the boss roaring in pain. My mind whirls with hope. I take a small leap of faith and glance behind myself mid-sprint. A cloud of darkness is spreading over the boss as its anguished noises grow louder. That's the virus. Holy crap, we did it! The boss will take a few minutes to be completely destroyed, so we have a head start to find the portal.

We really have done it. In the face of death, we have turned the GameMaster against herself.

CHAPTER 20

Because Ada and I are right next to each other, we wordlessly agree to be partners and take a sharp turn into the maze. Before entering, though, we say one last goodbye to our friends. This could be the end. I feel like everything that needed to be said was already said, so I stand there quietly and give each person one last hopeful smile. Rory and Ada exchange only a sentence, but their expressions speak a thousand words.

The maze is almost identical to the endless stone hallways, except the walls don't reach the ceiling. We'll be able to hear one another yell when someone finds the portal.

We keep to a steady jog, breathing heavily, peeking down each turn in case the portal is hidden in a little nook. I make sure Ada isn't overexerting herself—virus or no virus, this baby is going to be perfectly healthy! Focusing on Ada gives me an excuse not to think about Jane…

or the possibility that we could very well die any minute. There's complete silence for almost twenty minutes.

Then we hear the scream.

It is the scariest thing I've ever heard—as if someone's heart is getting ripped right out of their chest. It slices through the silence, tears through my ears. I clamp my hands over them, trying to dull the sound, but nothing can block out the anguish in that scream. It lingers, then dwindles to a horrific screech. This is almost worse than the first scream; it scratches my eardrums like nails on a chalkboard. Finally there's a feeble squeak, and the room is silent again. Silent, but screaming with the sounds of death. The worst part is knowing I'm not hearing some stranger dying. It is the familiar voice of our kind, loving Luna.

No. Not Luna. Anybody but Luna.

How could this happen? She did nothing wrong! She was the kindest person to ever live! This can't be real. This can't be happening. Not to Luna.

Crosby's desperate wail sounds from the same area, then I hear his broken-up sobs as he sprints away from the virus.

Our sweet Luna. She's gone because of that disgusting traitor.

The virus is getting closer. We have a few minutes, at best, to find the portal, or we will all die.

I do my best to erase the memory of that scream from my mind, and Ada and I race on, faster than before. We race through the hallways, desperate for a sign of the portal. Our panic translates into more speed as the seconds pass. Time is running out. Every second brings the virus closer. I feel the urge to burst into tears, but I resist. If I go down, I'm going down fighting.

Another yell pierces the air, and I cringe, afraid I'll recognize the pained voice of another one of my friends. But it's a different kind of yell this time—a yell of hope, desperation, and encouragement. It is the yell of someone who has discovered a portal.

"It's Rory and Sawyer—they found it!" Ada whispers. Her barely audible voice sounds amazed. I gasp in awe. Maybe there is still some hope we'll get out of here alive. I grab Ada's sweaty hand and take off through the hallway, the continued yells of our friends guiding us.

The only problem: now we are sprinting towards the virus.

The hallway in front of us turns black and crumbles into ashes right before our eyes. I skid, taking a left turn and trying to navigate back to the sound of the guys yelling. My fear is the only thing keeping me on my feet. We have seconds left. Seconds. My labored breathing soon turns into desperate gasps for air as I try to pick up speed. I can't go any faster, but if I don't, the virus is going to destroy us.

Using the little breath I have, I urge Ada to hurry, but the footsteps behind me suddenly stop. There's a quick yelp, and I hear Ada fall to the ground. Desperation fills my voice as I scream for her to push through and get up, but it takes no less than a second for me to realize that she isn't getting up.

She's unconscious.

It's either risk both our lives and possibly not make it or leave her behind. It's an obvious decision.

I *never* abandon my friends.

There is no time to think—not about my physical state, not about the virus, not about anything. With a burst of adrenaline, I swerve, hoist her into my arms, and keep running.

The virus is gaining on us by the second. Everything behind us is crumbling away—just like my strength. Every time I almost reach Rory and Sawyer, we get cornered by the virus and have to make a dangerously close escape. I'm already down to my last bit of energy; I don't know how much longer I can keep running. I'm stuck in this loop with no escape. Except, eventually, I'm going to run out of pathways that will get us to Rory and Sawyer.

The pull of the virus is too much. It would be so easy just to give up. No more running, just peace. But I can't do it. I have to keep going. I owe it to my family. To my friends. I owe it to Luna, who spent most of her life trapped in the prison of this game. I can't let the GameMaster and Jane win. My legs are aching, my mind is shutting down, but somehow I keep running towards that yell. The virus has destroyed everything mere feet away from me. It is closing in like a lion stalking a helpless gazelle. But still, I keep running.

I see one last open pathway leading us towards the portal, and I book it with everything I have. If the virus beats us to the portal, it's over. I can't let this all be for nothing.

Rory comes into view, and his eyes widen at the sight of us. He is clearly terrified; I am holding his entire world in my arms, and I'm just about ready to collapse. My vision begins to blur, and I stumble as I run. I gasp for breath between strides, my inhalations sounding like I'm about to die—which, to be fair, I might.

The virus is about to overtake me; Ada's weight is just too much. Rory sees what is happening and starts to sprint towards me. Why is he going the wrong way? The virus is right behind me! He skids to a stop, then scoops Ada from my arms without a word. In my exhaustion, I almost drop her, but he manages to hoist her up in time. Without her weight, I pick up my speed. Rory is close behind, screaming in my ear, but I can't even comprehend what is happening, let alone what he is saying.

My entire life flashes before my eyes. Everything is slipping away from me, and I can't do anything to stop it. All I can do is keep running. The portal is flickering, as if it is just about to disappear. But I am so close. The last ounce of strength bottled up somewhere deep inside me, strength I didn't even know existed, floods through me and I almost make it into the portal.

Almost.

I am feet from the portal when I realize that Rory's pounding footsteps have fallen behind. I whip my head around to find him inches from the virus, which is viciously ripping through everything behind him. His face is exhausted and desperate, but he has the most determined look I've ever seen. I am frozen in place. I don't know what he is about to do.

All of a sudden, it clicks. And at the same time, it happens. Rory stares me right in the eye, pleading with me to go along with his plan. He then glances down at Ada and gives her stomach a soft kiss. He brushes a lock of hair from her eyes and gazes at her face with love in his eyes. Then, with one final grunt of exertion, he tosses Ada towards me and stops running. I manage to catch her.

"It will buy you time! Now go! Please save her!" he screams as the sounds of the virus grow louder. Tears flood my eyes and cascade down my cheeks. No. No. Not Rory, too!

Rory gives me one last smile, and then he turns to face the virus. The smoke immediately overtakes his figure. He grunts and yells but I drown out his cries with my own desperate screams. Maybe if I scream loud enough he will come back. Maybe if I scream loud enough I can stop the staggering pain.

I am sobbing and screaming, but I know what I have to do. I can't disappoint him and what he died for. I have to take Ada and go. *Now.*

Of the hundreds of challenges I have faced today, none of them compare to leaving one of my best friends to die. I would rather have been wounded by the boss a thousand times over than have to go through what I am feeling at this very moment. It is the hardest thing I have ever needed to do. I don't know how, but I manage to take Ada and run.

I can't even focus on the searing pain in my muscles; my guilt grows and grows as I get closer.

I'm abandoning him.

Five more feet.

He could have lived if it weren't for me.

Three feet.

I've ruined the life of their child.

One foot away from the portal.

By the time I get there, I am a sweaty, sobbing mess, but the virus is right behind me. I have no other option. I hurl myself and Ada into the portal.

And although I am deteriorating both phys-ically and mentally, a small, hopeful realization crosses my mind: the plan worked. We have escaped *Escape the War*.

Falling. I'm falling. Again. This is how I started my two-year-long journey. A journey that has brought me so much and taken away so much. A journey that taught me lessons I'll never be able to forget and left me with baggage I will carry with me until the day I die. A journey that—as much as I hate to say it—I *needed*. It all started like this, and it's ending the same way. I feel the familiar pain of crashing to the ground, and although I'm consumed with guilt, I'm filled with grief, and I've probably just broken several bones, a smile spreads across my face.

I'm home.

EPILOGUE

"Chad, quit playing that stupid game! You are *addicted*!" I joke, mocking his twiddling thumbs on the controller. He laughs good-naturedly, and makes a few snarky comments back. Chad is in *love* with this new video game, *Escape the Maze*, and he's barely spending any time with me while I am on college break. That's just how middle-schoolers get when a new game comes out; they never look away from the screen.

Deep down, his obsession scares me, not that I'd admit it to anyone else. After I came back from *Escape the War*, my parents considered institutionalizing me, and I don't really blame them. Talking about living inside a video game—it's enough to make anyone question your sanity. My mom thought it was trauma-induced delusions following my "abduction."

Instead, I was sent to therapy. For an entire year I tried to explain what happened to me, but no one was buying it. Eventually, I gave up and pretended to realize that it was all in my imagination. At least I still had my friends. They didn't think I was crazy, because they *knew*.

Now, Ada is living with her little boy—who is four and a half!—somewhere in Washington. After Rory's death, she sort of shut down. She just stopped *doing* anything. It took the entire crew of *Escape the War* veterans to convince her to start living again. She had a baby to take care of! By now, she's more or less come to terms with it. I'm so grateful that she doesn't blame me for Rory's death; my own conscience blaming me was bad enough. I'm okay now, though.

Most of the time.

Sometimes I get nightmares replaying his last moments in my head. I'll wake up screaming, begging for it to stop. That part of *Escape the War* is pretty easy to hide from my mom. I usually say I had a recurring nightmare from "getting kidnapped." It haunts me. No matter how much I try, I know I'll never fully be free from my guilt.

Crosby is now living with his girlfriend (yeah, I don't believe it either), and both Sawyer and

Jaclyn have stepped out of the public eye and started living quiet lives *away* from the press. That's all I really know about their post-game lives. We don't talk much, but despite that I have a stronger connection with them than I do with my family. It's just—they *get* it. If I have a problem, I go to them. It's like they understand me better than I understand myself.

I miss Rory and Luna every day. Their deaths were the most traumatizing part of the game for me. They were my family—and then all of a sudden, they were gone. It's like a nightmare that I'll never wake up from. Thankfully, the crew is always there to comfort each other whenever we are missing them a little extra. But the pain is never going to go away.

"Listen, I'm only on break for two more days. I'll be back in school by Thursday! Better spend time with me while you can." I wink and nudge Chad playfully. We negotiate about quality-time activities for a few minutes, finally settling on seeing something at the local theatre. He agrees to go watch a movie with me in half an hour. We shake hands to seal the deal, and I leave to go get ready. Once I've changed out of my pajamas and fixed my hair, I scroll through social media until the clock strikes two. Then, I head back downstairs, my car keys in hand.

Maybe he will let me watch that romance movie I wanted to see... Oh, who am I kidding? He's going to insist on seeing the new action film. I don't get it; it's just a bunch of stuff blowing up. I reach the last stair and call out for Chad.

"Buddy, you ready?" I ask, twirling my keys. No answer. That's odd. I check his "man cave" carefully, making sure he isn't pranking me. Nothing. I check the bathroom, the storage room, and the guest room in the basement, but still no Chad.

"Mom! Have you seen Chad?" I yell; she's upstairs washing dishes. She replies that he is playing his video game. I trudge back up the stairs to ask for more details.

"Sweetie, that's all I know! The last thing he asked me was if he could get this pack that lets you 'live' the game. With his birthday money, of course. I said yes, but honestly it's such a waste of money!" She sighs, scrubbing a frying pan intensely in her exasperation. I freeze.

"W- what kind of pack did you say?" I ask, afraid of the answer.

"Something that lets him 'live the game'; I don't know. All this technology stuff." She laughs, but quickly realizes her mistake.

"Honey, it's fine! Chad is *not* inside a video game. He's probably at John's house. Don't let me ruin all that therapy!" She lets out a nervous chuckle. I don't reply. Instead, I walk robotically to my room, close the door, and sit on my bed to think. She doesn't even bother to come after me.

The soft sheets bring back memories of crying into them the first few years back after the game. I clench the blankets and try to release the fear and fury inside me. I fling myself back onto the mattress with a solid *plop*, my outstretched arms conveying my agitation. There's a light knock on the door.

"Honey? Are you all right?" It's my dad's deep voice. I pause momentarily. Should I let him in?

Since I came back, my dad has been the more understanding parent. Always respecting my boundaries. Always there when I need to talk. But it's not the same as it used to be. It's not like before. He treats me like I'm about to crack. Like even one joking insult made out of love would make me burst into tears. It's like he doesn't even know me anymore. Let's be honest, though: does anybody?

"I'm fine, Dad," I say quietly. It's silent for a few seconds, as if he is contemplating whether to leave. But, sure enough, his slow footsteps fade away from my door. I let out a long sigh.

I take my beaten-up playing card out of my pocket and slide it between my fingers. This is what I took from inside the game as a token of our memories. It's become my comfort object; it calms me down whenever I need to think. And I *really* need to think right now.

Chad's obsession with the new video game. Buying a special pack to let him "live the game," then suddenly disappearing. The only explanation is that Chad has been transported into the game. Just like I was.

How will Mom and Dad react? It was hard enough that one of their children was abducted for two years. And now they've lost *another* kid? The police would think that's suspicious. I have to convince them what's really going on! No, I can't; I'd end up in a mental hospital for good. Forget how Mom and Dad will react, how am *I* supposed to react?

It makes sense. Jane said that the GameMaster was going to make an unbelievable comeback sooner or later, but at the time I dismissed it. I thought Jane was just trying to justify her horrible betrayal. I can't believe the GameMaster is actually doing it.

My phone beeps. It's a text from Ada. I grab it eagerly, but my smile falters once I read the message. Her son has just gone missing, and he's been playing the same video game Chad was playing right before he disappeared. The beep sounds multiple times, each time signaling a text from one of the others I escaped with. The texts all say the same thing: a family member disappeared right after playing the same video game. I rub my temples wearily.

The GameMaster couldn't destroy us five years ago, and now she's going to punish us by trapping our loved ones in her new game. Because we defeated her. The GameMaster can't stand to lose, and we beat her. She's going to make us live with the knowledge of what our loved ones are going through and our own helplessness to rescue them.

After all, what *can* we do? Even if we try, it's a few of us measly past-players, up against a team of world-famous programmers. We can't outsmart them! But, then again, that's exactly what we thought before we escaped *Escape the War*. It may not be likely, but we will try! We defeated The GameMaster once, so who's to say we can't do it again?

I am not backing down from this fight. I'm going to rescue Chad, no matter what. The GameMaster is back and ready to play. But guess what? So am I. And so is every single one of my friends. The GameMaster may have found a way to beat us, but this is not just one battle, it is a war. A war that we will escape.

And we are armed and ready to fight.

ACKNOWLEDGMENTS

Words cannot express how grateful I am to everyone that has helped in making my dream a reality.

I have to start by thanking my parents, Rachita and Atmaram Nambiar; also Amma, Dada Anoushka, and Rufus. You were a huge part of this process, and I could not have done it without your constant encouragement.

When I began writing this book several years ago, Angelina Berg was by my side during the entire process. From reading my early drafts, to gossiping about character dynamics, and even discussing major plot twists, you have impacted this novel, and me, more than you know.

A big thank you to Nancy Gee, Publisher of MacKenzie Press and Laurie Blum Guest of the Re-Naissance Agency for giving me this incredible opportunity. You made it possible for this to happen, and I am eternally grateful for all of your hard work and dedication that went into this.

Thank you so much to my incredible editor, Katie Bircher, who with your help turned my 30-page story into a completed book with over 200 pages.

A huge thank you to Ilan Sheady for bringing my visions of Escape the War into the beautiful art that is the cover!

And thank you also to two of my wonderful teachers, Mrs. Repsch and Mrs. Pegher, for your support and encouragement.